A Book

of Verse

by

AV Samant

Published in India by:
AV Samant
Flat No. B4, Greenwood Meadows,
Candolim 403515
Bardez, Goa

First published 2019
ISBN 978-93-5351-130-2

On Par In

This Bazaar

*"Let my sentence come forth from thy presence:
and let thine eyes loke upon the thinge that is
equall."*
Psalm XVII, A prayer of David
The Psalter of the Great Bible of 1539

CONTENTS

ജ 1 ഐ

Skies blue were soft like easy days past greens
Of placid dew, sans another sign there,
Everything beneath the faint mid morn moon
Seemed calm as though everything was fine there.

And when just work cemented breaking days,
Their time believed that if done well maybe
Seconds made one with past's trauma undone,
Those year long instances would combine there.

The heart passed through hell, pleaded to the skies,
Stepped 'cross discarded, broken shells of hope,
Fell to fear, crawled out of long ago where
It had thought that it had built a shrine there.

The moving shadow crossed the worlds and

stood

At page's edge, the story's stage from where

Asked time if life played here in hour and toil,

Or out there in happy sun and shine there.

Ignorant, childlike of the thing called power,

The day then took exception to the hour,

But at twilight, to skies, it did confess,

That it may have been quite out of line there.

Last days of the bazaar unlike the first

With the sun, the new crown that reigned o'er all,

Then harsh its grandeur, now turned to receipt,

And skies aged by the colour of wine there.

Then the heart was born to partake in all

That took place those turning times of want

When moon and dusty dry, the rain and sleet,

The sun and stranger sat down to dine there.

ೞೞ

꩜ 2 ꩜

'It's right ahead,' said strength, 'few steps away,'
'Just give it one more try': the weariness.
Strength, when each road ran right into the sands,
Threatened to go awry: the weariness.

Solitude by the sea on seconds scorched,
Walked on unwelcomed, parted from its time,
Fell back, yet knew but to move on, not stop,
Nor turn to ask, 'Lord why, the weariness.'

Beyond blinding sunlight, the sky's pale blue
Told the hopeful heart that only it knew
What lay ahead, but its comforting hue
Was harsh and way too high: the weariness.

But the night would come, and the day would ease,
Burdens would be placed by the head to sleep.
The next day's road would return, with it

bring
Its needs and would supply the weariness.

Beneath the night, the rising peace closed
eyes,
To seal within respite from day's hard work.
End yet unreached, life had till then defied,
And it could still defy the weariness.

How oft in this world, the sun and the moon
In their unflagging hope, arisen, set?
Flegling weary heart thought their beauty
knew
To live on, dignify the weariness.

Limits were turned to frontiers of its world
And fatigue used to retrain and reduce.
From meagre was made its manor and thus
Life learned to occupy the weariness.

ॐ

ଛ 3 ଓ

'Was there a problem,' when questioned the
face,
Its doubt looked without still unsure, whose
fault?
And if there was, no words said there
wasn't,
How could one then find out to cure, whose
fault?

Mud path by the ocean to crumbling heart
Its rough way still maintained through
lashed by storms,
Year-battered and endangered, yet it was
Forbidden to take safe detour, whose fault?

Incessant rain, the seas thrashed shores and
skies,
The wind and birds fought rains that would
not cease,
When tumult fought strength both did try
withstand
What each could no longer endure, whose
fault?

The life of one's dreams did exist, they said.
And miniatures of the real were seen,
And their pithy descriptions too oft read:
Thumbing of dream's well-worn brochure,
whose fault?

Sit not to bemoan thy singular fate.
Life of thy making exists past this gate
If there lie waiting torments that secure
Tumultous lives of action pure, whose
fault?

Kaleidoscope   of   life's   uncertainties:
The shift of shape with each new sleight of
hand,
The well known pattern reflected again,
Encertained one could not ensure whose
fault.

ഃଔ

ℬ 4 ℛ

'Fall in love with me,' the day said to night,
Since in love lies death, and you lose yourself,
The night refused for it knew from before
In death lies fear, and so you choose yourself.

The dream was blue, but bright, tinted with gold
Rejected itself to future unfold.
Dangerous deception allowed to live:
'Fool yourself and from pain recuse yourself.'

'This should not do, no, but why should it do?'
Get up and move on for 'naught does appear
Out of nothing,' so you scream at yourself,
For dreaming, also you abuse yourself.

Another flower struck by love awhile
That withered up soon, curled brown, and then died,

If love gave this choice, to dry or to die,
Choose not yourself instead excuse yourself.

The new sun threw its shadows 'cross the lawns
Dark'ning old hours in display of its strength.
'Disappear again, reappear so strong.'
Lord of this world, how you amuse yourself?

'It hath newly begun, this life, old son,
To those that hath lived all along n'er died
Could challenge not the heart now newly tried,'
Saying thus, from action you lose yourself.

೫ 5 ೪

'You there, yes you, with no face or story,
Here, you! Try stay on par in this bazaar?
For they that went before you made the
mould,
That measured who you are in this bazaar.'

Wilst on haunches the next opinion sat,
Tapping tobacco gratis, handling acts
With each word certain only it knew best
What would take you on far in this bazaar.

Each new deal was made as the coppers told
How losers bought the next new secret sold.
Sun fell aclatter in the steel grey sky
Then silence rose as star in this bazaar.

Beside the till, same old tale shared anew
And voices snuffed that spoke just of its ills.
Tell not its halting lies, for if you will,
Sounds, its old voice, will jar in this bazaar.

'Twas not fair, but when living lives the flair
Became that needed forwarding the past,
And newly searching for that leather face,

That ancient hate helped spar in this bazaar.

The high hand and way through that knew
of you,
Which each speech knowledged, yet each
eye ignored,
For it could count each wing of flying flocks:
Power befitting the tsar in this bazaar.

The dearth that hath not the silver nor
strength,
The problem that knew to survive at length,
The fight, the talent, the mistakes, or them
two,
Knocked as they raised the bar in this
bazaar.

ॐ

6

Newly won the road looked around to find
Staring back long lost and wide-eyed was love.
Bound up by the shrubs of time and rebuffed,
All tangled up in thorns of pride was love.

The horses drew on cobbled streets a hearse
That slowly passed by folks who saw within
Rocking side to side on beir the coffin.
Shrouded, inert, and dead inside was love.

Time cared not that cruel hour cut branches,
Tore the leaves, dug the roots and killed the fruit.
It cared not hidden in the tree that died
Still red within the leaves that dried was love.

With real power none, only heart, heartless world
Looked on helpless its wisdom fall apart
It made mistakes, yet alive and active
In lonely place, a poorly scribe was love.

The feeling cut in two, in each more grew,
Into tiny bits of sense cut some more,
In smiling, wrinkled eyes that said it tried:
What life found it could not divide was love.

The hand would not put paper to its pen,
Or patience would not hold out might against,
And strength would not get past long work worn hours,
If not always there by its side was love.

A sustenance none handled governance
Request that starved first, then asked to be fed,
With wherewithall none but the will of God,
And that which would last though well tried was love.

ಔಜ

ॐ 7 ॐ

Archaic ink brightened and from 'neath the
dust
Plaintive demands of long dead scrawl, got
worse.
Winds of time blew pages past, shewed past
love
And then the call of its recall got worse.

A blazing hour had scorched a placid earth,
And shaken immortality that did
In last hours surrender, yet wondered how
It all occurred when its downfall got worse.

One long sorrow had got too hard to keep
For how long to wail, how much more
to weep?
When came the next, fatigue let former go,
Not just because its wherewithal got worse.

Heart lost track of time and it did not hear
If outside it thundered, or roared outside.
Days within felt fine, it cared not whether
Out there improved or overall got worse.

It never faltered so think of the shock:
The only time, like some heart, the mind fell
In love, then to stand, recover its poise,
It tried, yet balance of that crawl got worse.

Not everyone gets everything, its true.
When everything pointed that way, it knew,
It would not get through for the strictures of
The words 'You are meant to stay small' got
worse.

When cracks were noticed in its solid
strength.
No prayers put for eyes to see through tears
That fell a ground o'er which the head
stayed bent
When wailing at this pretend wall got
worse.

❧☙

ऊ 8 ई

The message slight brought in the breeze at night,
When shadowed by gigantic moon, it danced
Its unconvincing dance, and moon washed heart,
Unaware of impending noon, it danced.

Though one was the sky, the other a lune,
When they said that once the sun made the moon,
The mind moved, yet to the celestial way
It found itself never immune; it danced.

Why in this dance was once free will so dead,
Each silver spoon birth given blessed breath,
Yet, life played its tune, making happy hearts
Proclaiming that curse was its boon, it danced.

Thus, when on this side of the orb it played
Sounds carried to where reason was to

breath,
And not here but there on shadows and the
sands,
And there on imagined night dune, it
danced,

A step up to the light, two steps away
When out of belief, it stretched, then it
swayed.
This dance of lying and dying of self,
Each day to its confusing tune, it danced.

Sun of the dessert ordered it away
To where was nothing there, but next, the
day
Whence as before did rise same sun to shine
On dark moss green of the lagoon, it danced.

ഛൽ

ೞ 9 ಡ

Lost chances sped across the walls of time,
As one by one, villages went past me.
Brightly lit warmth within raced rocky cold
Without, but they both did not outlast me.

The country vast held no home from the
start
When young life left arms of its home for
good,
As time walked on, the mind kept up slow
pace:
'Care not I for those that have surpassed me.'

Made of mere flesh and bones yet stronger
made
Than smoke and steel that wonted not for
naught.
'The time wherein I lived to use was mine,
Though Janusine it did try outcast me.'

A teasing dream appeared then
disappeared
In this way that life would indeed pass me,
I stared stunned to see the dream approach

o'er;
Stood staring as it again bypassed me.

Did hubris think itself the lord of time?
Did nature make it party to that time?
Did pride need control of rights to that time?
When illness just hoped, 'Please don't forecast me.'

Carefully coloured as the tomes of past,
The word presented to be understood
By the time, it reached 'twas accepted ill.
Word said, 'Fie to thee. Thou hast miscast me.'

ೞ

ဆ 10 ଔ

Though clocks struck slightly later, the nightmare
Was up by then, already wide awake.
Through the panes, on squinting eyes sun rays fell
That sent the night to bright outside awake.

For long had been asleep, the life that meant
Being alive now that later would mean weep.
Till then, time would not allow life to fall.
Its call kept alert by its side awake.

Life's regret crushed by poem's pithy words,
That bloodied by the fear of being heard,
Waited till the scream had died, and for fear
In the stifled throat to have cried, 'Awake'.

The dream was needed to be realised,
Its spirit to not splinter, crash or break,
Eyes needed to keep shut to keep alive
The dream now that had long past died awake.

Stand thou up, small creature, and stand up tall
For though once life meant feeling small 'twas then,
Now new hope looks out to the morrow's call,
New babe still small, guiltless, wide-eyed, awake.

'Would it ever be this bazaar would fold?'
Thought this heart just another heart beat old.
One day it would know why all this occurred,
Till then it needed to abide, awake.

ೞೱ

ⷶ 11 ⷷ

It was the day that trod a space unsure
Between two moments frail and thin, it changed.
The tensile strength of time was sealed within
That seemed the same outside, within, it changed.

Could a heart tell whether this change was true
That knew naught else, but to receive the hate,
To shield the hurt, to love and lose that world,
White, brown and blue, true to its spin, it changed.

The orb that swirled to swell the waters still,
Time tested, rusted made the moments fall,
Yet as time fell freely straight in through space,
As myriad drops on water's skin, it changed.

Life, with sounds like seconds, off cobbles

bounced

To respair from decay, near dying growth,

When drumming of the skies bowed down
to earth,

When sun returned to weakly win, it
changed.

The season changed and for once life felt
fine,

Soft breezes blew, the sun bided its time

From now till twelve month hence, when it
will be

Time to welcome this season's twin, it
changed.

ॐ

୧ 12 ௨

A hell exhumed by exhaust and by fumes
When through the decent and through dry,
it spoke.
The bird chirped on quite unheard and
unseen,
In this world long past caring why it spoke.

How angry was the dream, and how distant,
Unwilling to bridge the gap it did seem.
When nearer, silence saw it was not so.
Therefore it waited, and when nigh, it spoke.

Life once said, you'll find that when time
passes
Will pass the chance to call the dream as
'mine',
And heart should speak when time it is to
seize.
To increase chances, tweak life's lie, it spoke.

A heart felt fine, in silence that felt 'mine',
But mind felt disregarded and ignored,
By the heart for its worth was felt through
praise,

Thus forced, the heart small with soft sigh,
it spoke.

Words told their tale as if only they knew
The truth by so many told two plus two,
Lonely and large silence said nothing more
It did not try or clarify. It spoke.

'In Poesy, truth' rugg'd royal decree
Did encourage that time's poetic work.
Written with thorough concern and with
care,
And though with acquiescence's ply, it
spoke.

क 13 ओ

To time new, like others, that day arrived.
How was one to know, no more, that was it,
That it would leave nothing behind to know
What would be, nothing to show that was it.

Time finally put forth rough hand with palms
All calloused, over worked, black, hard to hold,
Which the day could have taken and moved on,
But then, it said 'Thank you, no,' that was it.

Where was it, there beyond ships, beyond seas?
Was it here safe 'fore currents of wild time
Or here and there, beside them all knowing,
But no one believing, though, that was it?

At dawn, was seen soft love's promising sigh
That needed to be realised, then kept.
Morning heart raced, and time moved on to noon

To where the night turned time slow, that was it.

Thus then after the three worlds had been seen,
Their songs sung, their stories heard, their tears shed.
World within was the new world left to try
For now where else could one go, that was it.

The heart would not believe though that was it.
If life meant sorrow, did love not mean hope?
Should one to wallow life, not follow love?
It would wait out the shadow, that was it.

℘℘

ॐ 14 ॐ

The storms never stopped, when the heart
was drawn
By the shielded comfort kept in those eyes.
Its weather worn road a moment halted,
When it turned around and slept in those
eyes.

On ancient tear drops remained swirls of
time.
Its colours retained and patterns preserved,
As eddies of life stilled on surface smooth,
Of each ill tear kept unwept in those eyes.

When the look turned harsh, fearful, and
unknown,
Its sharpness caused once happy heart to
move
From its warm place of comfort wherein
such
Distress it could not accept in those eyes.

They say this sea is deep. It may well be
For one can't, but its stormy surface see.
Depths to be imagined here can be seen

For real nowhere except in those eyes.

Heart it was that went away, then came near,
Stuttered, fell short in folly of its fear
Of seeming stupid that it did just that,
And ended up quite inept in those eyes.

What place hath love's fault in love's
poetry:
The hand that turned for the sake of high
rule,
To stains of blood mark on brown staring
face
While ago by foot stepped in those eyes.

ೞೲ

৯০ 15 ৫৪

The odd time when the road got way too smooth,
An easy ride lacking stress, it improved
With obstacle new, a breakdown or two,
Life returned to rough road, yes, it improved.

Heart needed a 'Yes', but they said a 'No'.
The determined dalliance rallied forth,
Even though life's guilt became more not less,
Even then, life, more or less it, improved.

The heart sighed deeper, lighter than before.
Its new depths discovered odd in a way.
The old, felt new, when differently worded,
New terms wherewith to redress, it improved.

A heart measured beats, all's well it did say.
Life a series of quotidian steps.
Then a measure was lost, the beat was skipped.
Off key, it didn't confess, it improved.

It certainly was a matter of doubt,
And it should have been much better
thought out.
What was needed: some more of not
knowing?
With more ignoring the mess, it improved.

Yet when survival would not stay for that
Something that meant nothing, just in the
way.
Plain love was not reason enough to stay,
Unless it meant more, unless it improved.

☙❧

ৠ 16 ৠ

'Onward to success, your fine time has come,'
Then the day new found new me in between.
Just me, my pride, lost time, and its failure,
And nothing else could it see in between.

Tides of stasis dealt daily in ransoms,
That ebbed and flowed to the daily nets thrown;
But when the better shore could not be found,
When found was just sea, more sea in between?

Storms on the oceans lashed heavenly wild.
Yet safe across glass panes remained their lies,
Watching winds clamly, such warmth and such grace,
Squalls safe past carpets with tea in between.

The pearly dream was soft without satin,
Regal without hues of lilac and sense.

It stayed incandescent across each line.
No velvet was found to be in between.

Whatever its palette, each colour swirled,
That sky's canvas calmly caught to its ends,
And by the mortal that wrote out stilled
days,
Seen and sighed o'er ennui in between.

But mostly 'twas about making ends meet,
When heart to keep body and soul each day
Used and abused to needed advantage
Time over worked charged its fee in
between.

ঙ 17 ଓ

Humpty Dumpty off the wall lay broken.
King's men and passers by, all shouted,
'Smile'.
Cap of dunce was put on the fallen one.
The next one put on the wall shouted,
'Smile'.

The air was still and the people were tense.
Freedom felt subdued with all on the fence,
When the youngest one not knowing the
cost,
Being way smaller than the small shouted,
'Smile'.

When it was over, the field had emptied,
People had left, and the dead had been
cleared,
In the silence, sounds of crying within
Each empty, fluttering stall shouted, 'Smile'.

When the mystery of life could not be
solved,
For it changed the moment it had been read,
While 'Miles' altered when read and

encountered,
While one letter moved, its call shouted,
'Smile'!

Lining of life was softness of wisdom:
Now used as refuge and now subterfuge,
Yet it wondered had it also at times
While holding life in its thrall, shouted,
'Smile'.

Sensitivity stung, sense had said 'smite'.
Words had been wielded to cut for the hurt.
Pages moved shewing the seventh said 'wrath',
To the heart enraged, its gall shouted,
'Smile'.

౹ 18 ౹

The disregarded ocean broke its banks
And presented its truth, once tame to me.
'You ignored me in my calm, now face it'
Reality, full force, it came to me.

'Twas unseen and rotted for years now seen
By all, past life now out for all to see.
Eyes averted, people said, 'It happens,'
Their words sounded like a cloaked blame
to me.

Excruciating   day   unfelt   instead
Calm and quiet felt as the more it thought:
'If you don't reveal it, you can't feel it,'
The less and less real it became to me.

When confrontation meant not facing death,
That's when the mind would tackle and face
it.
It would be the day fear and real were one,
The day they'd feel one and the same to me.

That day though, life was a pile of grey ash
Whereon, the sun had shone way past

midnight.
In nightmarish light, in that subdued skye,
Horizons new became quite plain to me.

Past was acknowledged the present ignored
Still stained with the same poison of the
past.
'Confront the skull, come to terms with the
bones.
Find strength to survive,' was life's claim to
me.

ॐ

๙ 19 ๛

The heart was told that it should be careful
And it was warned not to go there, it did;
And looking right at what it was being told,
It walked on and fell to the snare, it did.

Heart knew to confess meant to be broken,
And though it knew it was already there:
Lying and dying, though now to confess
Would create the unneeded scare, it did.

Priceless trust was china forever crashed,
Shattered blue and white, scattered on the
floor
In still patterned bits, where the hazy day
Found it forever destroyed there, it did.

Real day felt upset to logic address.
Yet refused to dream it or to accept.
'What happens, does for a reason happen',
It tried life to find one thing fair, it did.

That forgotten wound though dry was yet
deep,
With its core still unhealed, and hurt still

sore,
That throbbed and surged, each time on the
surface
Life occasioned another tear, it did.

Heart being a heart was unable to side
When sense fought with sense, to protect
itself
From shots shot by each now disguised as
heart
Grudgingly it entered the fair, it did.

ಕ 20 ಜ

Came morning light when the moon rolled 'cross night.
Life easier found that the strain had reduced,
And as sun crossed the sky, twilight discovered
The day pretending its pain had reduced.

Those times meant just taking recourse to words,
That reduced one's self, inflated one's verse.
Writing improved, only when importance,
Belief in purposeful gain had reduced.

One's life improved, not when the times improved,
But when strangle hold over thoughts such as:
'Love was as poor as the reading of it'
'Grief and joy were all in vain' had reduced.

It watched the sun set, moved back to its way,
Unaware of what would be the next day.
Road at day's end, onward into the night

Turned 'round to ensure sun's reign had reduced.

Feelings were fossilised words in amber,
Some heart felt of life million years ago.
Read today, felt likewise a millionth thence.
Nothing it couldn't retain had reduced.

The stranger's foot appeared covered with dust,
That parted a way into the day's throng,
That as time passed was concealed by the crowd.
Barking restrained by its chain had reduced.

ജഝ

ਞ 21 ಋ

The burden was to be cheerfully borne.
Was it because strength in heart's core was weak
That it did falter, or was it because
Strength of the light burden it bore was weak?

Now it's such that all is lost to the heart:
No home nor hearth, makes one stop and to think,
Whether it should have gone out in the storm,
Or stayed in safe till its furor was weak.

Hate lead to hurt, hurt to hit, hit to hate:
Which lead us to where we ended up then.
It could have stopped there, but with one more hit,
Angry power within to ignore was weak.

Broken body just large enough to house
The heart only if its head lived apart.
Alone within the heart kept from the world,
That made sure its pain to restore was weak.

The song created to learn how to sing,
Which was elevated to the world's swing.
'No,' the heart said, 'Learn on,' but they said
'No.'
Their consent to heights of new score was
weak.

The strength of the body yet to be felt,
While the strength of the soul in body dwelt.
The heart and its mind had been long
o'ercome:
Their influence o'er life therefore was weak.

ೞೞ

৳ 22 ৳

The coin was tossed, it tumbled way up high
One second there, it tried to pin the air.
Then, back down to earth it toppled again,
No answers why it could not win the air.

Colourful butterflies and birds are fine,
Coins haven't any wings are made of mine,
To share space with one of another's kind,
Just isn't done. It could ruin the air.

The waves in rhythm, bobbed up and then down
To the ocean's beats drummed up by the winds.
On lonely shore, the heart found it could not
Measure to last night's grief still in the air.

Who knew if what they said was what should be?
Whether wise not to at times disagree,
When construction on its destruction lay,
By one's climbing the clouds to skin the air?

With restless, yet unmoving time pressed down,
The day's thickened life stood entirely still.
In that deathly silence, the heart did wait
For needed if slight breeze to thin the air.

Air of the world and of the heart within,
The heart's world and the people's world were one.
If of fine sense and sound was world around
That same sound and sense was within the air.

ಸಞ

೫ 23 ೬

Scribble of two plus two will try get through
The thing with a heart that was labeled
'mind'.
With free formulation, calculation
All crossed by an angry enabled mind.

No more wild flowers there in memory
where
They could be seen like stark transparencies,
That was where the wild monotone was
found
In a skeletal, trapped, timetabled mind.

Each thought could be seen out walking the
streets,
Each hidden fear seen round the corners
dark.
Each dream was first enticed and then 'twas
cajoled
To be destroyed all through a cabled mind.

The day centered round the noise of feelings
That tripped and pushed out the needs of
that hour,

The heart searched for silence pushed to the
edge
Of the crowded, cluttered, work-tabled
mind.

One day, it was said that wall will meet wall
The gates will be opened that will be all,
Until then time stood silent, obedient,
Fed and looked after in the stabled mind.

Look not for sense in words that were writ:
Laments of heart wherewith writer hit.
Instead sneer and jeer, deny and dismiss
These lines as scourge of the disabled mind

ॐ

௳ 24 ௴

Ups and downs of hills went past to give way
To vast view first, the blue breeze of the sea.
The rough and ready road slowed down to find
This life more languid with ease of the sea.

Head played a heart, and the heart played its part
As the burning sand was stripped of its shade.
Knees on the ground to the sun all around
Invoked by repeated pleas of the sea.

Bright broken pieces of love half covered
By the rocks, the shingles, the rippling waves;
Through open fingers of hand, sinking sand:
What awful wonders were these of the sea?

Road was waiting its rider had strayed in.
Far away from the rough and the ready.
'Come live life fine, finding presence of

mine,'
In nowhere near the degrees of the sea.

Call of the wild from on high and afar,
The moon wrote in water's ripples below,
That needed new sanction from the day's
sun
That freed the evacuee of the sea.

Too stiff will be return, too stern the turns,
Too tired a mind grappling acceptance
And spurn, but all beside that feel and find
Even though nothing one sees of the sea.

ॐ☙

❧ 25 ☙

Was it love or some such thing less sublime?
What was the way to know just what it was.
The pen was put down, the mind gave it up
As being lost for quite heavy thought it was.

Do you see in this: a grief, do you think,
Unknown fear, or worse, a conscience
unclear?
Why try make sense of life experience
When an incoherent inkblot it was?

When emptiness stepped in light like a leaf
Through doors left open to let in the breeze
A while passed before it was sensed then
searched
There, dried and curled, beneath the cot it
was.

Enough was it, the heart felt that it was.
Then, what about the thing to heart denied
That eclipsed fate, single strife that was seen
Could one unsee it, quite a lot it was.

Was   each   relation   a   celebration

Of cruel heartlessness and of conquest?
Afraid, hidden beneath its thin veil feared
Obvious heart whether or not it was.

The sun changed shape into the moon e'en
that
Played with the heart and shifted with its
time
To leave the day battered with vague sense
that
Life was left better, and somewhat it was.

White moon did rise upon the bazaar still,
All sleeping 'neath its whiteness and its
stains.
Accusations of pretence made that day,
Wondered from which colour begot it was.

ॐ☙

੤ 26 ੥

'There was much to do and then so much more,'
Mind urged the body not to slow down now.
Later, some day, life would the baton pass
That held the day and could not throw down now.

At last, round the corner a sound was heard.
Heart thought was it the foot fall of that time.
'In time, that time will come or not,' they said,
''Twas for the heart to learn to bow down now.'

Day dragged, its feet made heavy by harsh while.
'Twas best to be borne out till its passing.
Know that the heart can and will soar in time
When sun shines through that seems also down now.

The minutiae of being: battles of life,

As in broken lamp or the dripping glass.
Constent amending will mean appending
Of what could be trivial show down now.

At times just watch, at times snarl, a menace,
Then an advance, maul, unexpected withdraw'l.
Predacious volatility, and yet,
Precious life's breath, 'twould not go down now.

Time spent to justify 'unasked for' life.
Birth that meant sanction of the one above.
Day's end at lonely table ill poet
Had to show life one more rondeau down now.

ೱ 27 ೪

Time passed to end each failed sentence's
life.
To keep its beauty, to endure, it tried.
By making past pen give present its form,
The formlessness of time to cure it tried.

Weak grasp of petal, silky, smooth and red;
Fresh green by approaching mud soon
destroyed,
The inky fall of raindrop nothing knew
When corona pink to procure it tried.

'Hold on to wakefulness, never let go
Into darkness, yet hold on to the light,'
As the night, pulled the heart unto itself,
The mind its senses to secure it tried.

The broken heart tried to present
itself,
With but impoverished pen could it put
forth
Its indulgent case to demanding world,
It could but try, and why, for sure, it tried.

'All things shall pass', said and all did too.
Perfect and imperfect also did pass,
Yet, mind turned them into a memory,
And thus to maintain the past pure it tried.

Stars flickered on high as the fire blazed,
The shadowy trees to its music swayed.
The heart watched the flames reach up to
the stars,
That with its charm, to win, to lure it tried.

Lurking within the shadows in the bush
Were nameless dangers that would follow
soon,
With glint of coppers two beneath the moon,
Failing health the heart to insure it tried

ಸಆ

ೞ 28 ೞ

When life made friends with fight, it carved
its way,
Since then it with fight did pay, forever,
And seemed as though not just till fortune's
sway,
Seemed as though 'twould be that way,
forever.

Small hand coloured large beyond petal
lines.
Child's art notebook paper seen by the ditch,
Unseen by adult hand, crumpled and
thrown
With its childish dreams away forever.

Traveler had brought a basket of love
With bread, cheese, meat, and fine flask of
wine.
The basket remained, weave of its maker,
The rest turned mem'ry of May, forever.

They say, thoughts are weak and writing as
well,
But the heart surely says it well this time.

One time maybe, when put paper to pen,
But how long would the luck stay, forever?

The skies rolled out as they do with each
day
Sporting another hue. To stall God's ways,
In 'Prince of Tyre', insulted, ignored
That sky was writ to be gray forever.

Each hand writes and above it another.
Words extended to finale unknown,
Ta'en for unknown reasons so as to last
What was ill begun that day, forever.

ᔥᔐ

ഔ 29 ଓ

Maybe discordant, yet time moved in tune
To the song short for a while when it sang.
Maybe mistakenly, the heart felt strong
And its life felt less fragile, when it sang.

The heart made large asked fast reducing fear,
Was it feeling fine and could it not hear
That it did not care, for it knew to move
Back and forth, rhythm and style when it sang.

Feeling by tune cut to pick up one more,
Thrown by the juggler that cartwheeled and crooned
While despair for now from the sidelines watched
The flight that seemed less futile when it sang.

Though two notes were separated by eight
Plus itself could not separate the hate.
Though the song knew not fear could it say that

Its low-slung notes lacked all guile when it
sang.

'There is more to life than har, har, hee, hee'
One wise, old, wizened woman rightly said,
Yet setting the world to tune now and then,
The heart walked another mile when it sang.

When shops opened, the industry began.
Worthwhile   folks,   buying   selling
worthwhile wares.
Till box of metal clanged often to make
The market place less hostile when it sang.

Too rich to sell, too poor to buy was what
Befell the heart displaced from up on high.
When it tried to sell itself, they said, 'No.'
Like its day was volatile, when it sang.

❀ 30 ❁

'Twas frayed at edges, and charred by the sun,
But because green and newborn it wasn't,
The heart could still live past a fly ash night
And dying, still say that torn it wasn't.

'Twas then the blind mists descended on days
And time took on varying shades of grey,
Awash by vastness, confusion 'twas when,
It turned quite dark, but withdrawn it wasn't.

In that silence still was that knocked down chair.
Screams that followed kept within the heart that
Took to the road, distanced itself from thence,
Telling itself that careworn, it wasn't.

What had it taken a tear in the eye,
Sigh on the lips, repeated avowals?
This world used to calling 'unseen' as 'true'

Could be well fooled that lovelorn it wasn't?

When life was steadied by love for a while,
Though life still fragile, the going was
smooth.
Heart said 'don't worry', as if 'twere in
charge
Of waters and being bourne, it wasn't.

Fie thought the heart when the temple
doors shut,
'Gainst it for reasons the good priest knew
best,
And though for awhile the heart felt as
though
From His love it was forsworn, it wasn't.

ೠ೧

80 31 03

In morning silence, maybe it would come.
Nights were waited out for morn to appear.
Next day went waiting at twilight hope said,
'Wait for it until next dawn to appear.'

'It existed,' the world despaired of love
That was wanted, but deemed not to exist.
Naïve heart still cuddled the dream, still yearned
For the unseen and unborn to appear.

It had said 'twould come, or had it, who knew.
One time that the prophecy felt so true.
Time could not dictate the sun, nor the king,
That dictate shadow and pawn to appear.

Distance stepped in that had looked from afar
In derision and heart shrank back in fear.
'Maybe, it exists', at last conceded,
'But quite brave that 'twould have sworn to appear?'

The heart roughed up with a black eye or two,
Scruffed and left to learn its lesson just taught.
Slept like a cat, in the box at it thrown.
In two eye's lines, dream redrawn to appear.

'Maybe because the old skin of last night
Not shed by new day, it did not appear,
Or because the next day's new and bright light,
The next sun had not yet worn to appear?'

ℰℛ

૛ 32 ૝

For long was it tied, to its reason fixed
When fin'lly came reason to shift from it.
Once shifted slightly thus once heart released,
How easy 'twas floating adrift from it.

The sea breeze brought in the swaying wreckage
Of a well-lived, perfumed, yet hidden past.
Who here could know of its follies and flaws?
They knew it not that had not sniffed from it.

What were the storms that happened out at sea?
Which waves met with what sort of currents there?
What was it that drew the waves back to shore,
The same had fled previously swift from it?

That boat was stranded grew circles 'round it

That managed only a rock to and fro.
When came a wave it moved a bit more then
Settled down again, got no lift from it.

The scum of tedium was stuck to its sides.
Even so there below a new world seen:
Greenish blue magic transcending dreary.
It accepted 'twould not be rift from it.

Bring them on, sinner, the hills are not done,
Like the call that echoes one after one,
To song sharp with each note finely in tune
Its loud eclectic got short shrift from it.

Thus, wrought jungle was forced to ride aback
The hapless, dirty, wretched, wild boar as
The shine of the Shah cheered on from afar,
Strange success that they had 'Josephed'
from it.

ൕൖ

ॐ 33 ଔ

Its well-shaped cousin asked the clod of
earth,
Misshapen and dirty, how rich it was.
From underneath its gold and well tipped
shoe,
It barely said, 'Impoverished', which it was.

'Twas night, their lights toasted the stars on
high,
And world below was shadowed by their
style.
The moon brought down to earth was seen
shaking,
Now shining, now shaking a-ditch it was.

What of threads as nets of bright mirth were
thrown
That caught those few stray feelings in its
weave.
As one fixed smile got mistakenly caught
Found unraveling fast in the stitch it was.

One colour so loud set others alight
Or ashade, both were by each one needed.

Midst crystal laughter as 'twas pointed out,
And then thrown out when shelved as keitch it was.

Far away there, good life bubbled and burst,
As a show for the heart that watched sometimes.
Yet, from demeaning dark to lamp lit arc,
Quite unable to make the switch it was.

Darkness and trembling lamp, paper and pen:
Peopled this corner musty, damp and tense,
Though cat's eye and quartz cut it from afar,
Yet able to wrythe in that pitch, it was.

₨⌢

❧ 34 ❨

Day was confused for though the night had
passed
Behind it, as stricture, its flack was there,
Past moon was though all gone, still dimly
lit,
Its old chanting, enchanting track was there.

At each step, the foot turned over a stone
To learn from the life forms that lived
beneath,
To gauge what weather would be further up,
And it said all what it did lack was there.

One shirt for the back, ragg'd shoes for the
feet.
Meager possessions kept all beasts at bay.
As for society, not heeding heart's need,
Made sure that its constant feedback was
there.

When the ripe fruit fell, half eaten by birds,
The flowers also died unpicked on each
stalk.
The path, though covered by overgrown

grass,
To old, ruined, beaten down shack was
there.

In flick'ring darkness, the poet that wrote
The approach of each new, upcoming
storm,
Dust was that poet, dust also that storm
His passage on paper in black was there.

After his death, all the poems were burnt.
Charred words were then scattered atop the
grave.
Where a skelet, permanent bent o'er work
And by overlords turned hunch back was
there.

ᮥ 35 ᮧ

Compassionate kindness, this time around
Heart wondered if it were a trend or not?
If just a trend, contemporary friend,
It wondered if 'twere doomed to end or not?

The dunes at times rose, at other times fell
In their path on way to heaven or hell.
Hell from where the high palms considered
it theirs:
The privilege to condescend or not.

Hands exchanged money, and the deal was
done.
Journeyman waylaid that needed some help.
Smile was in place and the dagger not seen.
Was extended hand of a friend or not?

At sharp cut of envy did it begin,
And end for certain at harsh turn of grief?
To mark out lost love helped reduce its
power,
And help hopeless heart to transcend or not.

When it came in the terror of the night,

To defy stillness, mock darkness of life,
Drunken uncertainty of firefly
Did its temerity offend or not?

Words came too many, and meter too short.
Hubris of writing helped tying of knots:
Written to be read if only to find
To some purpose would it extend or not?

The father and son spoke not the same word
Or they did and other meaning was heard,
Also when high priest spoke, how could one tell,
The turn taken was a godsend or not?

ॐ 36 ॐ

The rare hour it was when the world ignored
Felt free enough to win that silent thought,
But then slighted, undermined and angry
Time returned to ruin that silent thought.

Where had it been, which universe milling ,
Sap of which starry essence distilling?
Mind clashed, clattered, captured, and uncertain,
Of new peace to repin that silent thought.

The silence knew that the night was quite crude.
Met with silence, the day also was rude.
If neither would let the other one be,
Why bother to begin that silent thought?

Where was it, who knew, perhaps in the words
Of bygone pages written out anew,
Gone with hearts deceased, yet echoed in minds
Of those alive, therein that silent thought.

Unspoken words knew, how loud the silence,
The power it had to shatter, and said:
 'Trust them when you fall entirely silent.
 Speak not, but stay within that silent thought.'

Trust and obey, so the black-white keys played.
Month of the mourning the heart did obey,
With palace of plenty replaced by trust
When was made of satin the silent thought.

ಸು 37 ಲ

The sound of thin mourning arose to rent
The death of the morn way out west, they
watched.
As each slow shroud was being carefully
placed
Upon each broken, bleeding breast, they
watched.

When just one voice spoke out against the
cause,
And when some more voices rose to oppose,
And then more voices joined, for or against,
And yet, as if 'twere all in jest, they watched.

Nothing was free they found with love
enough
For each one to begin to fear both lives.
Paid for their love with their lives,
whereafter
Each heart slashed and put to the test, they
watched.

News after news, the sphere drew blood for
blood,

Anger for anger, hate for hate, but then,
Respair would follow the gore as they said,
For the while that they let it rest, they watched.

The hearts were heavy and the eyes kept down
To get past themselves, the day and debris.
If one met uplifted gaze whilst at work,
'Twas quite quickly averted lest they watched.

Child like in love, aged in the fear of it,
Once alive lovers learnt feelings to fear,
If they left love alone: they were left alive,
If left alive seemingly blest, they watched.

☙❧

ಖ 38 ಚ

Night passed to a day break quite beautiful,
Yet by evensong, twilight was better.
When less was sought, a lot was brought to
night
That day and next, when the light was
better.

One wondered whether this day could have
been
Thus achieved through just daily strife and
strain.
Although each day, its daily work was fine,
One does agree fortune's sleight was better.

A life, now white in dark, now dark in white,
Interspersed with too many specks of light,
All poised, but who could make it out at all,
Now that, night gone, morning's sight was
better.

One more impatient colour burst the scene:
Now red, now blue, now pink, now navy
green,
Though what was seen's yet to be believed,

E'en then what had been all right was better.

Instantaneous eclipse into darkeness,
The meaninglessness of world had drowned.
Thousand strong words of robust sense instead,
Impending death or some fright was better.

'Easy times, show not thy skills, in the face
Of life that knows to smite the strongest foe.'
If life turned easy through show of times' strength
Given time, some lax, its might was better.

☙❧

ೞ 39 ೦౩

The mind was put to test of time for though
The day had past still militant it was.
Faced with world's call to let go or redress,
Cost of distress, exorbitant it was.

Time passed by, when life was quietly spent
Yet minutes or its seconds seemed hell bent
To make the going rough, yet this constant
Taking stock, life, an irritant it was.

There in the growing crowd intellect
feigned,
Here in the silence, feelings were arraigned,
One spoke, heads turned, isolation broke by
Words whereof now participant it was.

They said that it was true, for they all knew,
Calculation brought things to better view.
Yet for a smitten heart to admit that
Two plus two was true, hesitant it was.

Days were uncommon, suffering mighty.
Words used were sudden, and yet, to fall
back,

Stay rejected, heart lacked 'je ne sais quoi',
Still, that time, quite impenitent it was.

What hell on earth: fires broke past which gates
Whereof the spirits made one wrythe in pain,
But now and then, cool breeze blew and becalmed:
Some relief, though intermittent, it was.

❧ 40 ☙

Soul waited nearby love's grave, awaited:
The final fear 'I'll give you what you want,'
But the heart that died also had waited
To hear: 'I will give in to what you want.'

The harsh words were yours, they were true,
of course,
And hurt feelings yours, yet, were they that
new?
Rejected, yes, but when the distance grew,
Mind repeated 'You'll get through what
you want.'

The charcoal promises were golden made
Into rhymes brought to be sold to the world.
'Where is thy weather. Where thy wheels?'
it asked,
'No? Then would you get on cue what you
want?'

Some money, society nothing brought,
Same sooty promises, but nothing new:
Old words like floating dust shining sun's
stream.

Did say, 'Turn this world into what you
want.'

Night was turned into the next by the word
That turned woes of dark into hope of dawn.
Back the sun rose, its owners knew better
That said 'Other than win, do what you
want.'

When warring good asked for help 'gainst
the sun,
When up on high, owner and priest seemed
one,
When doubt and fear asked for help he said,
'Sure,'
'But know you cannot undo what you want.'

ॐ

ಸ 41 ಛ

Gentle came the words: 'Keep a base
beneath,'
'For it will be of help when you fall, love.'
And gentler, yet 'Do keep a little ground,'
'And be sure to never cross it all, love.'

'Go on, just take one little step, try walk
Away from this and try to walk towards
What may make thee miss a step, fall to
death?
It might, but that's no reason to stall, love.'

Unknown it fed on endless discomfort,
And sheltered its unseen hate and kindness,
Smallness would prove to be way too vast,
but,
It said, 'Vastness might be way too small,
love.'

When were heard plaintive calls of the new
you.
Again the yearned for signs of the true you.
Long silence, nothing heard, and then again,
There, it was, if so, why fear its call, love?

In this, the place of changing shapes, one face
That had changed to love then, now changed to fight,
Whereof the same hand heart knew as caress
It would get to know to hit and maul love.

Love, thou slave of emotions, that lasteth
The worst of wars, liveth through basest want,
And learns to sail harshest sea, through frailty:
How holdest thou this world in thy thrall, love?

☙❧

ॐ 42 ൙

The heart muted then it realised that
A good side had sides of bad beside it,
It would be safe, it thought then and
remained,
With no way out curled and crawled inside
it.

Storm swirled the certainty of life, thrashed
ease,
Blew safety of norm and known, exposed
death,
And stepped across the world, watched fear
of dearth,
As the colossus that stood astride it.

Out of what was thought good, the bad was
made,
But confusion made from both good and
bad.
Within was the warmth of winter's comfort,
Yet life raged on, love raged on, outside it.

High above was creation's cranial dance,

To melody of endless, madness mean.
The heart found itself tiring eternal
Of shine, wine of pride that did preside it.

Of course, conditions improved outside it,
And fair weather returned, and beside it,
Life might have improved had it not to make
Up for that till then had been denied it.

'Delude not thyself thou art deserving,
Oh heart that sets complaints in hard, grey stone.'
Then did the hapless one retract protest,
Childlike again asked the lord to guide it.

ॐ

ॐ 43 ൠ

Blood coursed, the head unsteadied, and
fear rushed,
In face of the unfolding force, again.
Like magnet to heart, part enervating,
Part strong was current in the course, again.

A sorrow once well known, returned all
grown,
And returned as contentious strength,
although,
The heart also stronger now with critique
Refused to give in to remorse again.

Listen now, to rustle of silk, touch now
A work worn shirt, feel now perfumed
velvet,
Riches spread comfort over fatigued love,
Such was taking easier recourse again.

As air grew heavy, and the time turned frail,
As the pointer shot up the richter scale,
The time, it shuddered, settled to a low,
Weakness tested strength in its source,
again.

Clouds o'er river's gush, mists o'er angry
hush.
If sport allowed the thrill of drowning, then,
Victorious hand to wet departing foot,
Why will not ambition endorse again?

Gold citadel to struggle past the pond,
Said, 'Time to get back to work's
subsistence',
To step down from a painting earn one's
worth,
And jewelled ambitions divorce again.

ಶೋಲ

෩ 44 ෨

Could it be the day had not weight for it,
Or the seconds had not the height for it?
A heart stood apart, not denied, they said.
'Twas just that the time was not right for it.

The quest lay outside caught in thorny shrub,
And strength inside imprisoned in the mind,
If the contest of life could untangle
Self from doubt, could it win the fight for it?

At the start of each day, it moved from there,
And crept slowly to where the prosaic weighed,
There it found the dawn not too drunk with brawn
And the twilight not too polite for it.

Passed years of writing in the blinding heat,
Lifetime of struggle, and lifetime's defeat
Through perfection of words that made no sense,
Past truth that always seared too bright for it.

The heart made it seem just like yesterday,
Looked back and found it was further away,
When 'twas all starting then, now 'twas all made,
To die next: that truth was not quite for it.

Rarely but the eye did clear now and then,
To see fine the down, veined leaf, shafted spring,
Layered lights, lathed nights, gold speckled dawn:
Creation was n'er too samite for it.

* 45 *

Could the heart clear guilt and not fear the
gold,
That it needed to walk to you, it would.
Could it clear the field and not fear the tears
Choked in tired throat, then that too, it
would.

World meant destruction and the villain
knew,
Yet sometimes also meant construction true,
Hope grew, life grew bare in its open grave,
Could ailing heart give death its due it
would.

Whirlwind, with its gyrations and its name
All coned in indulgence, for sure, it came.
What noise, if one could hear the master's
voice,
The heart would certainly get through, it
would.

The walls of houses were long gone in
grime.
Overstepping time, tales were long past

shine.
Now aching head rested on future dread,
Could mind's eye bring it into view, it
would.

White vines would grow, curling up
terraced sides,
Desolation's desire and comfort slight.
The moon would surely accept it as need,
Though white night of feelings untrue, it
would.

The mirror on the wall shewed flower slight.
Was it frailty or first signs of might?
Though, life certainly meant to brown and
die,
Moonlike, if death meant rise anew it would.

ಏೞ

❦ 46 ❧

At the end of day, could it move away,
Or should it stay, learn to adjust instead?
By this new movement, new beat, and new
fear,
It stood, how should it learn to trust
instead?

As waters shifted, the waves drew back
sands
To melt foundations of retreating steps.
Just as life settled down in eddy next
Back onto the shores it was thrust instead.

It turned out, what was needed was given,
To it by the night of the day that won.
If the day's excesses were deemed as true,
A night's injustice seemed more just instead.

Who knew feeling if loved, would show
worth?
Who knew it would show awareness if
owned?
Who knew that the shackles of love if shed,
A birth would replace the disgust instead.

It was at noon that the pink sea breeze
whirled,
Such noxious salts hurled in the far flung
lands,
That the station moved on this far off shore
And still life became wanderlust instead.

Was this story begun in media res?
Then for what reason did it turn round
To the start, and all that had till then passed
To the end it did readjust instead.

€ 47 S

The day napalmed, the night before was calmed,
Finally now the feeling bad was gone.
Ev'ning neared turned daylight to ticker tame,
At least that feeling, now be glad, was gone.

In wined windows, shadowy darkness reigned.
Stark heavens thundered, security maimed.
First the intermittent thundering sounds
Appeased and then the flashing mad was gone.

Walking guiltlessly away from that place,
Competence seen, the mind could not believe.
Next day, experience began to learn count,
Till the part it could not add was gone.

But then, hilarity burst in the head.
Soft lights bubbled, sleep rose to reign instead.
Liquid sounds poured laughter in the

silence.

Pure fun now that the dialogue had was gone.

Darkness mellowed harshness of neon haze.
Near cup shimmered, and far off music blazed.
Beyond it all, it was still there, all there.
Day found only what was dream clad was gone.

Time would not dissolve, heart took to the road,
Where each thing went no sooner than it came,
One moment a mem'ry, next it had passed,
With it what the high ones forbade was gone.

ॐ

ೞ 48 ಇ

Life ahead was thought to be free from snares,
If it could, through chance, surprise you, it would.
If the way ahead could the facts belie,
Show distance as nigh, then that too, it would.

With its loving, word pleases, with its smile.
Through imports unseen teases from within.
Not ever to be owned, and yet e'en then,
If future could keep it in view, it would.

Shadows were underfoot amidst the fun,
The throbbing lights danced and dazzled as one,
If calloused palm could catch moon's shadowed spot
That night mistakenly let through, it would.

Now there is this, tomorrow what will be,
Will it change, and will distant fortune strike?
Will life gain or be just like this, the same?

Could ignorance give heart a clue, it would.

Was believing just dreaming between days,
One day more before it died, turned to grief,
If love could add a day to each new day,
And deny life and death its due, it would,

This poet, a slight dreamer and no saint
In possession of more words and less sense.
'Midst pithy plaints that rent his clothes
one more:
'Would word desecrate what was true, it
would.'

**
 49
**

'Twas caught between tomorrow and this day,
The heart needed to breathe and place, to move.
Between 'What is' and 'What can never be',
It had to somehow make the space to move.

In slim stream of light with its floating dust,
The harsh darkness never had prettier seemed,
With fortitude was borne the night that closed
In to stay and had not the grace to move.

With what was, for a while, for now, between
Two seconds in this space that made the mile,
Could there a way be to pass ennui,
To cause inert, unmoving pace to move?

Between the 'this here', beyond the 'that there',
Could there ever be, what the heart did see

Perfectly in mind's cluttered collection,
Though the doubts it had to misplace to move.

The move began gradually, steps first walked,
Then quickened into a deafening run,
Foot to foot, shoulder to shoulder, all one,
A surging tide, one human race to move.

When uncertainty brought frailty and being
Rooted to the spot felt better than not.
With the house all broken and safety gone,
Misgiving it had to embrace to move.

੭ 50 ੲ

Blinded love stared dry eyed as to whether
It should first try test fickle fate and see.
Later, it would, perhaps, give way to tears,
But first it would hope. It would wait and
see.

A needy word did speak to ask for love.
As expected it got its desert hate.
A lesson learnt this reversed world hears
straight,
So 'twould ask instead for some hate and
see.

When the business was tough, with options
none,
Decision came enforced, with time that
knew,
But to run past light never to return,
'Should one then bargain the rate and see?'

One does agree to sit and wait out fate,
Maybe way too long, maybe far too late,
Yet, e'er hoping, waiting for fortune blind
To shift at least awhile its weight and see.

Each picture worth a thousand words unseen,
Each word just thousandth part of picture big,
But word forgotten, when the nervous hand
Coud not dissemble, illustrate and see.

When the new had dismissed all that was known
Which was then replaced with the new unknown?
When given chance, once denied heart did think
With noise it should set record straight and see.

ೱೲ

ૅ 51 ಚ

Boat rocked by life that went on dead ahead.
Could one say of its life: it earned nothing?
When was left behind, debris in its wake,
Could one say then its life returned
nothing?

Once sodden page where written words
had dried
Half washed away as stains, wherein tried
days
Reflected past floods, experience whereof
It found it neither gained nor learnt nothing.

Up the tall tower constant breeze unkind,
Chimed on and on nonstop to its own tune.
Tinkling, talking mind, senseless back and
forth,
Cutting dry the air like it yearned nothing.

Past the walls, the sounds of hidden fires
raged.
Life gauged the destruction there from this
side:
It seemed safe as though at the gates the

blaze
Turned ash and died, as though it burnt
nothing.

And so there was the clue, what came in
threes,
Would not follow two by two, love did try,
And yet the answer firmly lay in lies,
For in what was seen, it discerned nothing.

On waters, life became the wooden barque
Worn out, tossed about which depended on
The turn of winds n'er good nor bad taken
When given for still chance adjourned
nothing.

'Is this gaol a ship, stormy wind waters.
Is static movement, and day's end the land?'
To take or keep you in place where it would
A sly, taciturn life externed nothing.

ಬಲ

ༀ 52 ༃

Desire unknown, held by the heart for long,
Seen far off for real, found that leased it was.
What had comforted o'er the firmament
Now said, 'The chant of absent priest, it was.'

Tree branches hung with greed were undisturbed,
Yet by life unseen, untouched, and unstirred.
Skies past the red sea sun was rent by cries,
Cries of that wailing, wounded beast it was.

Came the dawn, 'twas pink and temple-ruined.
By noon its face would be to sun exposed,
It needed to be time smoothened, for yet
They found just risen, still night creased it was.

This then a story unlike others old,
Yet each one felt it was theirs to be told,
Star so long 'neath that when it first appeared

Described by ones waiting out east, it was.

The tale had at long last been narrated,
Whereafter each eager bird flew back home.
Relentless push put the horse back on road,
Its tired story though long ceased it was.

When few notes of that ancient tune were
heard,
The heart jumped, yet the mind knew not
the words.
The same, yet changed o'er time, to fit the
new,
In whiche'er form, still sung at least it was.

Far 'way from home the well worked mind
lay down
In that same state it thought it left back
home,
In a new world below, but that same sky,
Whereby same stars on high policed it was.

ೲಐ

ഇ 53 ര

The lies, those fat ones that liars knew best,
Truth be told, that they really knew few
well.
Knew they better, ones they already knew,
While lying, defying they would do well.

Between them, the grass of distance once
grew,
Manicured by the guilt of people few,
Past love etched nothing, up there in skies
blue,
Fair flowers smiled, they both knew that
view well.

When sepia seemed not too dull nor brown,
When altered gravely by depth of new
times,
Modern day, its strength gave to age its
youth:
Faint, well-meaning, pale, bright hues came
through well.

Lights dawned as black pieces of time now
lay,

As tattered carbon light on helpless hand.
With care the day started, in the hope that
It would be that rare one to treat you well.

So it went on, an ageing body spent
Each new day that also aged, one by one.
Mind sat back to watch the latest twilight
Reliving all that went down not too well.

Upright gaze saw naught past the temple
doors
But doubt and confusion and haze and
haste.
At night, the broken bod knelt down in
prayer,
And then it felt it knew that Jesu well.

ॐ

ॐ 54 ॐ

On surface of life it stayed calloused, dead
As sign of past life, past shikar of love,
That hurt no more but 'neath it was as if
Just struck, a hurting new won scar of love.

The orb, its blazing heat felt, nearness lost,
Its anger terrified, and distance gained,
As it passed near, further went, more it turned
From heat into a point sized star of love.

Balm was blue, they said, the ointment would burn
The while it took to cure. The test was true,
They said, as potions plied their worth, heart hurt,
Near death newly drew tabooed jar of love.

Death became a reason to die, as though
Desire for life proved too alive a task,
When life was learning to live out love's lies
Then o'er again those feelings mar of love.

Enough, now, love does not exist, does it?

Felt it once was, not felt it once was too,
If it did, they knew, they killed it and said:
'Now, don't show how guilty you are of
love.'

By public, peopled out to solitude,
To poverty, chastity, obedience,
And inability to turn a Fra,
Heart stayed this world, a blue boudoir of
love.

Heart watched the parade ta'en out again.
The trumpets blew and the drums struck
their beat,
The skirts swirled and the trousers strut
their best
And teased and pleased in fine patois of
love.

₨ 55 ₢

At day's end, pine pricked eyes searched city's haze
Though lost, it knew, its distant view was there.
Failed mind lay down and put itself to sleep,
In breathing said 'Its acrid clue was there.'

If mind cleared, the still mired sun obscured
Branches and the heart, as collateral,
Seared to death: a birth, destruction, and dread:
All that the tree had to go through was there.

Was graffiti the boast inscribed in scorn,
Or blackened pride cut too deep in bark's edge?
As redundant and residual life
Remained, yet green frisson slight too was there.

Whatsoe'er it wanted, the world despised,
And had it not, would all wanting have ceased?
So with this train of thought, heart made its

peace,
Because its basic need, it's true, was there.

What fate is thine, worshipper of the word:
Thy step knew not at the next what would
be,
That schooled its heart to turn blind to the
hour.
Death's breath that spoke till then to you
was there.

'Does life live only for comforts and scores,
To keep itself safe from its enemies?'
It learnt to read the word, to trust the book,
Till then fate and whate'er it threw was
there.

ॐ

ੑ 56 ੒

Where was it ta'en, to whom, for what
reason?
Of dangers, the mind tried to know ahead.
The heart remained blind, not needing to
know
What lay hidden a mile or so ahead.

Bright future seen, first steps were gifted
keen.
Happy heartbeats danced out their day long
tune.
Next morn the young heart first saw its
ageing,
Then worse from itself that lay low ahead.

Sharers of space turned silhouettes against
The red controlled infernos of their time.
Leave they might later, but for the moment,
They stayed sum and substance also ahead.

The heat increased, more strife marked the
rough road
Passed underfoot, as had done for those
dead.

Callow, the green heart tried waiting out time,
Creating its own softer glow ahead.

'Not now, not the time nor place to sit out
The fight to wait, to rest, or to relax.
Restlessness raged, forbearance failed, time moved,
Let fatigue and faith lead the show ahead.'

Faint sunlight came wearing veil of waters,
Soft and slight breeze in turn coated the coasts,
Eyes had becomed veined like the stress of storms.
Joy would surely come dressed as woe ahead

A lightening bolt was held by slight wrist,
With wristlets removed to ease driven pen,
As poet's guise was put on by the pig
That could not compete with Sappho ahead.

ಹಇ

ॐ 57 ॑

Something stupid of no consequence found
Quite ripe then when what else got lost in
time.
Blinkered innocence found lost like old love.
Discoveries accrued as cost in time.

Rootlessness firmed, isolation turned norm
As time grew up reality turned stark.
Warmth of the story got frozen like thought,
Its blood stilled and crystalled like frost in
time.

Small feet, bless them, had cared only for
dust,
When foot jostled foot in young, aimless fun.
When that same firm foot now fronted foot
firm
On two accursed paths that got crossed in
time.

The heart allowed eyes to feel that old
warmth
That had died in that era turned to new,
New coldness, growth, independence and

eyes:
New eyes it would have to accost in time.

Both good and bad then too were tossed in
time,
When each one was given an unknown
theirs,
What fell there, for over here, there fell fear,
But good and bad then too were tossed in
time.

Hand of the father, hammered and chiseled,
Broke the glass ceiling, turned sky into steel
With gates placed unseen, its world locked
and barred.
Cell of the heart numbered, embossed in
time.

ೞ 58 ಞ

With incessant plaints of the heart ignored,
A mind assured that so much more was heard.
In the city amidst the noise and rush,
If listened to, the voice of yore was heard.

Blurred life rushed past windows, rhythm and rails
Clacked out new and steady invites of death,
Yet, by this roving, e'er transmitting frame,
An intermittent keeping-score was heard.

Lightening had been struck across the bough,
That cracked and crumbled to the ground beneath.
Near death had to regrow green in its wounds,
Before what progression was for was heard.

What voice spoke and who believed the voices?
Could they be explained, if not, then what spoke

Through starry death of painter's night and life?
Was it the same voice that in awe was heard.

Only after the child was born and died,
Still a babe, the flower fin'lly faded.
After they had gone, faded and silent,
Wisdom of all that went before was heard.

Live and then die in the manner prescribed,
That asks thy suffering so they can live.
Small fist in the manger moved, cattle lowed,
As voice of the sage Melchior was heard.

☙❧

ఈ 59 ಇ

When the word was said to mean just one thing,
They thought it would not convey naught to them.
Heard and seen, past the warp and weft of hate,
It appeared skewed, appeared a knot to them.

Joke, some chuckle and tease, all made to ease,
The stress of life and harness on its freeze.
Now, what if that was mere relief to us
But then, 'twas conveyed as such not to them.

A florid style with two lines too many,
Some gravitas, too much of little sense.
But, viewed with doubtful mind, it's true, that 'less',
Could have meant more than 'not a lot' to them.

At each step, the hour was stymied, further

When shaken steps began to wonder why,
That at each turn, a counter turn so neat,
It began to feel planned, a plot to them.

Hardly any times for respite and love.
In those, really, love prefers battles not.
One ended, next began, heartbeats whacked, yet,
What use saying, 'It had all got to them?'

The past moments had gone dressed in their drab.
New ones arrived, fresh and fine all in fun.
Not once rememb'ring the fathers now gone
As though it mattered not a jot to them.

The old came back as the new and the young,
Past sorrow returned recovered as fun.
Narrow thought widened and spread like the breeze.
Faults were found in what had been taught to them.

₧₨

ॐ 60 ॐ

Tapestry of trees and seas seen through mists.
The fumes, had waters and fires spun it?
What's full- grown now, began long time back.
Which ancient, sometimes shaking hand begun it?

How long to last, what lengths of time should pass
To get to this new-found then from frozen?
Just few futile miles of the game were done,
And the fool, a pawn, thought it had won it.

Seconds, their smallness stretched, to put more life
Into life than just a living, and yet,
When small hours were turned to sane seconds large,
Then time knew that it had overrun it.

Essence of chaos creation endured,
In fine pursuit of some well-timed technique,

But conquered, not by the mind, it remained,
As formlessness, yet how could one shun it?

Hatred of earth knew itself as hatred
Of self same ones made of stuff of stars,
Yet with escape none from earth and this self,
Suffered the while it remained upon it.

Around that time composure dipped again,
When strength of legs turned to unsteadiness,
When muscle of the world had slapped again,
Forbearance knew it had underdone it.

Life's storm that arrives no precaution brings,
Gathers no clouds gather, turns no weather in skies.
Trials would have been easier borne had loss
Ignored all warnings that had forerun it.

℘ 61 ℘

Time survived this way: when came the new morn
It was born, when came night it killed itself.
Living the moment and working the day,
'Twas in routine's way that life skilled itself.

The grey cliffs of impatient days, loomed large,
Large was the need, to see past and beyond.
Seeing eyes turned golden, day's vines were grown,
With fine thoughts the blind mind's eye filled itself.

As failure drew each time each image new
In life's guidebook, by each experience learnt,
It showed the heart how to fall and feel small.
Then to crawl, grow tall the heart drilled itself.

At each day's death, the evening silent fell,
When the old man stood up 'Courage' to

preach,
Emboldened stars came down, settled amidst
The stories told, creation stilled itself.

The night lengthened the life of each frail lamp,
As shadowed traveler by it lay his cares.
Way too plain had been the day, so the night
With silver cicada sounds trilled itself.

Pages of the book kept aside were turned
By breezy fingers showing black and white
Nurtured not what red heart sought at such times
Joys of His world not word tranquilled itself.

ॐ 62 ଔ

Blank white of the day splashed with stains
of greys
From past when by mistake, it had said it.
When the night was seen skeletal and
charred
Apyre, the heart began to dread it.

Was fear of unknown or unknown of fear?
True, where there was one, there was the
other.
If not, no sooner one arrived, it seemed
The other one was ready to wed it.

Resignation was not in the stricture
That to spare the rod spoiled the world of
guile,
Resignation in that the hand that hit it,
Was the one that cared, nurtured and fed it.

So what, the word wrong stood with the
other:
The word that was once in its meaning false.
More doubtful 'twas then, than had been
before,

When first the eye of critique had read it.

Is perfection, thing other than failure,
Or perfecting continual past defects?
Success is now in disgust of its past.
Does it forget its defects had led it?

The heart had found its pride and lost its peace:
Its world became fields of the hunted prey.
Fine farmland turned burnt scrubland of past love
Killed o'er by the same life that had bred it.

Those brought to the brink by upheavaled life,
They say turn closer to Him that made it.
Beleaguered, and then steadied by His hand,
Heart found way of life to softly tread it.

℘☙

ೞ 63 ೞ

Sleep searched moving skies that moved
with the times,
Rolled in crude nights and chased the sun
away.
The just awakened eyes wincing daylight,
Shunted fearful dreams just begun away.

That time when the thought found no open
sides,
No meaning to turn to, no place to hide.
Looking out its prison bars, it could see
The purple tree, but could not run away.

Rhythm of metallic sights, back and forth
Went the clashing of iron days and nights,
Time clanged into place, and life's track was
moved,
Pushing grief that had weighed a ton away.

Beauty of path there was none other than
The sense that someone had been there
before,
The heart gazed upon its memorised view,
Long after life took that someone away.

The heart pinned under the day's severe
truth
Turned happier with some soft, home-spun
lies,
Relenting a while to the heart's desire
Then time took the lies it had spun away.

Hand tried on both sides of the line to coax
Eternity to futil'ty invoke.
Time could only be caressed and captured
For awhile and could not be won away.

Forever downed and floored, when well-
being crawled,
In the happy rule of the queen of bees.
Hit to near death some many years before
Fight could not mend the damage done
away.

೫೪

❧ 64 ❧

Mind liked coherence, each thing coherent,
And turned into a lucid thought of words.
But, it found feeling was made of feeling.
It could not be made out of a lot of words.

There was deceit, made out of many words.
Guile was wordy too, hatred also knew
That beyond time, was a love made up of
No one yet knows quite what, but not of
words.

Quite sordid 'twas to punctuate the blue,
To write the heave and wave of ocean's hue,
To want ethereal glint of drops of dew
Written on this tangible knot of words.

Each word said had depth of unknown
layers
Wherein the poet unwittingly drowned.
If each, naive word writ could kill times o'er,
What would be of this lethal shot of words?

Hubris was this blue ambrosia of ink
To outlive death by marking frailty blank,

Whence Herculean labour build proud castles
On this quake-prone and four lined plot of words.

Proud words were writ and the writer interred.
His papers collected deemed to be doomed,
Apocryphal verse, not to be believed:
These spurious, heretical trot of words.

For writer's life had nothing earned but scorn,
From morn to morn, till the ink dried again,
From dawn to dawn, when as proud pen had posed
These ungraded, injected slot of words.

ல௸

₨ 65 ⅚

If naught were by it, but denial's strength,
How entirely on its own it would be.
Small boat afloat on still ocean, fragile,
How tough, trivial, and alone it would be.

Thought, if it knew what made false and what true,
And what it had meant when nothing made sense,
In a lifetime of learning, achieving,
Unlearning of certain tone it would be.

Heart saw enough as the myriad flowers fell.
If to each it knelt down to turn guilty
Each and ev'ry time to colours aground,
Quite uncontrite and unknown it would be.

Who knew things would be this way, way back then
When alive on hope and when experience
Had it proven that whatever came next,
Glut or dearth surely on loan it would be.

Heart made to rust, to turn hard, build a

crust
For if it remained that way, soft and swayed,
Decidedly dead, no tear left to shed,
When in the next, new storm thrown it
would be.

Winds went away, the heart did stay shaken
To witness its devastation a ground
Through which it rummaged, through each
piece in hope
The way to live onward shown it would be.

Now dearth hath changed the limits of
fatigue.
Long crossed was the length it thought it
could go.
Heart recalled the times it thought to itself,
'Relax, else worn to the bone it would be.'

৶৹

ೱ 66 ೲ

Rose, its disillusionment, a fragrance
Threatened to say, 'Now, just stay out of it.'
Once out, disbelief was the gift opened
To say, 'Now try find a way out of it.'

By life killed, but not yet dead, turning cold.
Death still hurt the bloodied body in bed.
Legs broken, yet alive, life stirred itself
To say, 'Get up. Walk away out of it.'

What kind of fool was he, to stand in court,
To make light of this dance, to give darkness
To those that needed light, to tell them that
'This final night, work, make hay out of it.'

Knees were bent, the clothes were rent, the
heart prayed.
Sight ahead seemed closer, firmament
shook.
Some hand shut down the inertia of life.
The moving road paused midway out of it.

Words of songs, 'cross hills, meant what e'er
they did.

If song sang 'delay', the heart only heard,
 'One day I will be out of it', and then
Affirmed, 'I will be one day out of it.'

But then, when feeling was left intestate,
Uncared for by joy, nurtured for by fate,
When it learnt to live from within itself,
It learnt to make everyday out of it.

When the world saw a purse where there
was none,
A crown of thornes put on head of the one.
And used for their needs while bleeding
heart tried
Walking and fighting the sway out of it.

ॐ

ஐ 67 ༀ

The terrain got tough, road steep, weather
harsh:
Dream damned as hope decided to leave it,
But some distance down, it did turn around,
Thinking that maybe it could achieve it.

There it appeared, that old season made real,
Beside all the dreaming, beside disbelief,
Beneath the sun, glinting shamelessly
When the eyes told the mind to believe it.

Spacious fabric of society and self,
Woven out of where an ennui dwelt,
When one hand held love, other worked
destruction,
And dissatisfaction did weave it.

The heart was kept, maintained far from
them all,
Divorced from all those who mattered too
much,
In midst of it all, its beat still alive,
If it could feel it, it would then grieve it.

Then all the while, the hand worked at the
loom,
Spinning rhythm and rhyme, and spooling
words
Of fine feelings and woe, yet awaiting
The final sweep of the hand to cleave it.

Its end when glorius soft light was seen,
Steadfast the heart felt world vindicated.
Mind turned to doubt when the foe did kiss
woe.
Heart had known: belief would not deceive
it.

When Time did not care much for the
moment
That loomed large, the gory ghoul from the
past,
That now rivalled, but what did it expect
When from dry, ancient vault it did thieve
it.

ಐ 68 ೞ

Yet, love as a game, it needed being told.
When its fun had begun to entertain.
Heart feared the demand to write of what went
That had been not much fun to entertain.

Seekers were not e'en a few, but just two.
Two way too many, yet smaller than one.
Village not of just few, but of a score
For whom life's lies were won to entertain.

Love thought the lover was larger than life.
Could one be larger than flowers, tears, and verse?
Love needed kindness though harsh at its heart.
Now that thought had been done to entertain.

Love or the lover, the choice was not tough.
Loving meant rejecting required world,
And rejecting meant denying each one,
Except one like the sun to entertain.

Write again for experience knew itself,
And its poetry spoke no more of flowers.
Love passed, world teared as it knew it had been
All a part of life's run to entertain.

In time of course on burnt scrub green fronds grew.
The deed of the day, to be wished away.
Needed then why for in future to die?
Each needed that some one to entertain.

Read not a meaning in any of this,
For this verse new born derides ancient love,
Love that's lasted like these words will not last
When nonsense there is none to entertain.

ঙର

ʕ 69 β

It was that time when past their silent stares,
Stories of strife and living one could tell.
In their silences, need to own their lives,
And yet certain misgivings one could tell.

When to be kindly meant to be quite weak,
When to be rude meant to be in control,
When kindness meant falseness and hatred
truth,
When a fear of forgiving, one could tell.

Not only did they not speak it, nor did
They e'en think it much less did they seek it;
In total sev'rance of their past, their need
To avoid its reliving one could tell.

It was that way that time, or seemed it was,
For who could say, why it was all perceived
That way, when its wisdom was imparted,
Nor was there need for giving one could tell.

So it was that full, fine rivers were scorched,
And turned arid, into dry beds of hate,
Yet in small, low pools of residual love,

Eternal hope's outliving one could tell.

Days worked their ways, and past time
became new.
The gone remained as stains in records writ.
E'en there, a trembling of certain writing,
The truth's certain deceiving one could tell.

Who could say what was true, what untrue?
When they said it was such, labelled as such.
Seen close in emerald finish of life,
Creator's constant weaving one could tell.

℘℘

स 70 ो

When it was still young, all raw, green and new,
Its frailty had been fun to entertain.
Then it grew into a tree bearing fruit,
Whereof lies had begun to entertain.

When the ladybird small-stepped 'cross the green
Towards the pearl blue drop of dew 'twas fine,
But when it crossed the grey rough of a stone,
Its drive seemed overdone to entertain.

The view, its promise, the dream, its promise,
Longing for the love, its uncalled for deed,
And all that fooled the heart to think 'twas true
Had been ten times now done to entertain.

The bird sang, sparrows danced, the leaves fluttered,
And the insects they just glanced in

boredom,
As the moon bid adieu and farewell to
Everything 'neath the sun to entertain.

Why live it, if not to be happy, why
Force life to feel discontent was that joy
That forced feeling for the poet a toy.
No more was that thought won to entertain.

That verse was once writ then written again
Like the life that was stuck in just one place,
Made slightly better when was no other.
The complacent o'erdone to entertain.

She would come round the mountain when
she would,
Till then what would be verve was
exhaustion,
And despite lord's help to keep her life held,
The people there were none to entertain.

ೞೞ

ॐ 71 ॐ

Belief, fertile as a thorn, like strength worn,
Yet this day was not to be long for once
Time turned and season changed, it would
return,
To become again as it was, strong once.

The old heart, adherence to resistance
It lacked with humility, but it knew,
That scorn was here to stay and would turn
vain
If rhythm and refrain turned headstrong
once.

Once, it pleased the ear, eased severity,
Lessened love's fear, and e'en then, what
would be
If the rhyme was left, where it had been
once,
Or else e'en there, where it did belong once.

Time changed, with it right became wrong,
and wrong
Turned all right to forget what was newly
Wrong and what invited the wrath of might,

Had been all right once and not so wrong
once.

Fortune's day did exist though not friendly
Willing only to being stared at afar.
The heart recalled, when of its own accord,
It had decided to come along once.

New day 'twas when air cleared and movement
Felt not so afflicted with fevered pain.
New day it was which fin'lly ended one
That had felt so endless, so lifelong once.

Yet people were happy, regimes were kind.
Food was plentiful and ample means fine.
No one expected or wanted again
What was written so well in that song once.

ॐ☙

ℬ 72 ℭ

How could the mind know what was said
won't last,
Though its weakness had tried to assert it,
'Twon't last beyond that line or that lifetime
Since there had been no sign to alert it.

On one hand a beating, the other praise,
Of the two just one can fill up the space.
At cross roads the mind left alone with none
To support it and none to divert it.

Were this heart believer, world would make
sense.
The clouds would clear, and the road would
be seen.
Pitfalls ahead prepared for in advance,
Meek enough to be able to skirt it.

In this world, trust was still cousin of love,
It was a way, the only way to go,
To trust an unknown, scarily unknown
For the heart was one way to convert it.

To be wary of trust, still not reject

Was an art which each one knew very well,
To co-exist, yet preserve oneself well,
Live out one's lifetime, yet not exert it.

So, just when the heart thought that it had learnt,
It tripped and fell into distance and doubt.
World wide wisdom was best left to the world.
The heart knew trust, 'twould try not desert it.

And then came the time to trust the temple,
When their slight and hit had harshly said, 'Stay',
'Twas time to stop talking and abide that
Which had hurt the heart to disconcert it.

ॐ

₨ 73 •

Warmth was a vigil and love was black barred.
The heart though all tied up felt feel free enough.
As long as it could look beyond its tomb,
Sunk dark in its sea, it would be enough.

Fate, the bully, saw its victim first fail,
Then fall to its knees, to plead moments last.
Her fearless eye silently watched its death.
Last sacrifice to her was plea enough.

Game was played well, and the loser was thrashed.
The stands crowned the winner as best, e'en then,
The podium was pleased when to its disdain
Success had bent down on its knee enough.

Though mind lost the heart to the lonely shirt,
Lifetime could satiate not abling greed.
It was said then, 'Givest thou me the world

And yet thou wouldst still not give me enough.'

Find the fool that stomps within the poet,
That shouts in exultation where there's none.
Words fade color, rhythm turns into tin.
When the fool has shouted in glee enough.

Heart distanced and denied was asked to leave
The conversation that wanted it not.
Quiet, it turned around to the soft sun
Wherewith its strong draw it could see enough.

The bazaar was its world, folks were denied
To it and its life in one corner dwelt.
The day was ta'en down to its dark quarter
In soft twilight, life felt mestee enough.

♪ 74 ♪

City bloodied, when the heart brought to mind
Crippling hurt, it felt sad that it happened.
Then memo it signed, the words memorised
'As experience be glad that it happened'.

The mind that fought the heart of blurred vision,
When its feet felt shaky as frailty feared.
Strength fainted, public square gods mocked as one,
'Is it down? Ah, too bad that it happened.'

No famine nigh with the dearth of enough.
Dry excuse of way too much for far few.
Repast laid out, not till 'twas first denied,
And then when it was had, that it happened.

It benefit some, hurt one, cries of none
Echoed by none, and now, to whom to turn.
The folks of the country said that it was
With reason ironclad that it happened.

Sun rose and it set, slightly unstable,

But not to worry, yet, just stuff of books.
What to believe: memory, ache, or fear?
'Twas within this triad that it happened.

Fool jingled thons hat, the child really cried
Behind the placard of tears, when they laughed.
In roaring applause, the last line was lost
When the actor did add that it happened.

Life dragged its legs across its crippled life,
Lord of all fates danced the figure of eight.
Word turned silent as some far off threat said,
'Fine man, if a sight cad, that it happened.'

Loving light healed, and the memory sealed,
Life turned placid if smouldering within
That emerged at times as few, worthless words
Then 'twas of this pen mad that it happened.

ॐ

ಬ 75 ಛ

Life gave some to one, more to another,
It gave fairly and equally never,
It gave sorrow, suff'ring instead of joy,
It still gave and was miserly never.

It happened so one time, powers were laid
To rest, the world got drowned in waters
thus
Came the wait for the day, next in the line,
One that would be fine, finally - never.

It was that bad or seemed so to the heart
That would die from faults of living and life,
Never know if there was a mind wherein
The courts were just and leisurely never.

'Poems celebrate the fineness of life,'
Said compliance to the poet too poor.
Meagre made fancy and put to the word,
In a way feted, usually, never.

If the moment wandered out to the world
So scorched that unless it worked it would
die,

In deserts, the shade needed to be made
That seemed to occur naturally never.

'Come, live the good life and learn to see what
Without which the good life can never be'
'It gives you what you give it,' there they lied,
'With no joy, life was neighbourly, never.'

Loud words they said, heard by all and the heart
Down and out needing a stretch of belief,
Pronouncements of life flavored as spice heard
Were made to be ta'en literally never.

ೞೲ

☙ 76 ❧

'Twas not needed,' they said, 'and neither real'.
There was no face to it or name for it.
When in time, it all did come to the fore,
'Twas then that the plaids took the blame for it.

Poet lived in the land of one with shoes
Too rent and hair made of the silk and sun.
The land of the poor too rich for the heart.
The land of the rich was too lame for it.

Fine was the life enjoyed by just few while
The ragged made do with them in their view.
Quiet bliss of barely making it through
That majority felt no shame for it.

To arrange the part distorted the whole.
To write the best was not always the goal:
Best possible not forsaking the soul.
The heart was given no claim for it.

'Don't discredit life,' earthly wisdom said.

Fascinating heaven, this tortured hell.
Could faith survive intact this harsh world
when
To play with trust was just the game for it.

Then came the day when last fight called life
out,
When forbearance lost, surrendered to hell,
Fevered with fatigue, legs limp, and it fell,
When Death's angel finally came for it.

If to end life was the aim of the fight,
Life's calm release would go down on its
knees,
But strength floored, yet it moved, still faint,
alive,
As though death was end way too tame for
it.

‱

ॐ 77 ॐ

To fate was born a moment unwanted,
When for some reason, luck deserted it.
Time gathered it up, starkness tutored it,
Towards safety, distance asserted it.

As beasts wild amused themselves with the
pup,
Bare storms found it lost and took its leash
up,
Tossed it around this way or then that way
And into their plaything converted it.

Aim of abuser was worth to reduce.
It made it first fall, feel worthless and small,
Then affirmed existence, set itself up,
Till to retraction fate asserted it.

A sharp mind helped its limp and its
stumble:
Its body broken by mists from afar,
To drag it through time and pray it would
not
Falter every time chance alerted it.

'Don't let that bastard learn to read or write',
Or fan fires of forces strong that are
Scared to shun the book that lay whereupon
Its name and spine, time inverted it.

When mind was given no weapons to kill,
To preserve self over and above self,
'Read to learn nothing, search to find
nothing,'
To this benign fate life diverted it.

And then from there on the tale was told
straight,
Heretofore hinted from fear or from fight,
That was Lord's creation and He knew best,
The strange plot wherein Life hath quirted
it.

Read on fair reader, try to forgive that
Resolve hath tried to indulgence avoid
With all its complaint, grievance and
protest
Until the folks' will hath subverted it.

ஸஐ

Ω 78 ℧

Distanced through time, brought together
by fate
To the crown born, raised by jewel it was.
Father against son, past with the present,
High with low, life, a long duel it was.

From up high a bird fell out the tree's nest.
It struggled amongst the brambles below,
Where torn and flailing, under the sun's eye,
Watching ruin, life's renewal it was.

There is 'method to madness' it was said,
And this direction never left its head.
All through life's madness it looked to the
sun,
Respaired through life's ways, like fuel it
was.

Their truth was thus confusedly seeded.
'Make thy bed and then lie on it,' they said.
Mind and the heart were abed with no bed,
Past hath no present unusual it was.

Life, for sure it came joined to another:

A name that it knew yet felt not the same,
When it thought to pick up those earlier reigns
It tried and failed ineffectual it was.

It was not what it thought it was but what
They called it, 'the long ago heart' now dead.
If this one was unlike what they wanted,
Too bad, what they wanted cruel it was.

'Twas late when the people sat down to sup,
Stretch of the bazaar saw not the same fate.
Luck of the good day made the meal better,
If not then, some rice or gruel it was.

Entire view was had not by the heart
That felt the billhook but knew not the cause
That prompted its use to cut down the branch.
Little it knew of sense dual, it was.

ಙಚ

န 79 ဒ

Heart must see without not within, it must,
Yet how can it just be a seer of life.
How can't one tell itself from self-pity
Egocentric, blinded by sphere of life.

'Kill ego, kill self,' in it pride doth not
See a thing other than it sees its death.
It forgets itself, and sees not the world.
It hates and lives in constant fear of life.

Still the journeyman walked on and on him
Each sorrow leeched, walked the woods, alongside
Him always, one more clung on fast and quick,
When the earlier one he did clear of life.

This life was hacked out in strange rough terrain:
False glade of glory fell from other skies.
Life crawled on this ground basking in that light,
That came from afar from that tier of life.

Why are things the way they are, if one can
Live out but its part, then the whole is known
To whom, who can tell where it starts and ends,
Who can say should one grieve or hear of life?

The clime was strange, its tongue was none too plain.
It tried to preserve what it knew at heart,
As 'now' carried forward a long past 'then',
As sad attempts robbed good Shakespeare of life.

Shaky pen affronted cuts of steel when
Survival attempted such imprudence.
Daily sun did set and these words were lost
When worst folly reached its frontier of life.

౸౹

ৰু 80 ৫৩

So that it could fall, to keep itself small,
The fraternal mind did actualise it.
To control, it had to give up control
Only then did the heart realise it.

As the pen was writing, its nib was smashed,
And white of its page slashed and streaked
with blue,
But the hand wrote on, stain drawn out as
words
By heart that went on to idealise it.

No, it was not that way, why should it be?
Them against us, was it, all pairs of three.
No, it was not, but 'twas me against me.
Thinking so, we did contextualise it.

If the world was 'prison and purple tree',
The eyes watched in knowledge it would
not be,
With present imprisoned future was free
For who here could not visualise it?

The truth of the heart seemed unlike the lies,

For if the lies were real, truth was untrue
That died for the people found it too harsh,
To speak of it or to eulogise it.

Derided by those that sat by the tree
Golden sunshine round wrists came not for free,
Or something of the sort for too tiring
It would be to think or analyse it.

The alter too high for one yet too small.
Come, be a choir boy, best, not at all,
For the good man did lathe, the warden stalled,
So heart then turned home to journalise it.

The world was in flux or waters in flood
That nothing seemed certain, no one felt safe.
No sooner the heart began to believe,
Than the good hand did immobilise it.

ೲ೪

ಋ 81 ಇ

Rumbling and noise of the words of itself,
Its depravations that life's notion made,
Were worse than upheavaled, once calm
waters,
Approaching storm sounds that the ocean
made.

Eyes watched the dancing silk shirts of this
world,
The heart felt coarse and quite drab in its
wool,
The mind turned that into that which it
wrote
Out dipped in blood's ink like a potion
made.

Shirt that was rent was one made of the sun
That shone a quiet million years ago.
Fools of the day saw the starch in its weave,
Unsheathed their knives and commotion
made.

Maimed and made lame it grew to the life
that

It neither recognised not understood.
It turned to the only thing that it knew:
Life in its mind whereof devotion made.

Turn away from worship, the page did preach.
Turn to that which the lord hath made thy task.
The heart looked at its grief gifted by God
And of it, its writing's emotion made.

Doors of the temple to the heart were shut,
Yet everywhere, He existed like light.
'Shut the last large door, open one too small.'
Thus newly challenged, its promotion made.

Battered once by the Lord of all fates that
Spoke peril from ev'ry face, ev'ry word,
Within and without against the heart that
Yet faith, Life its tenet 'precaution' made.

౸౹

෨ 82 ෬

The heart, market loitered, by temples sat,
Like locals, yet found that it fit nowhere,
Unlike cobbles rounded under bared feet,
Estranged, yet remained a secret nowhere.

The quill was inked and the order was
struck
That replaced the shaky scrawl of the scribe,
By the wrist and its flamboyant flourish
That ruled and could place the poet
nowhere.

When the moon had fled and the night was
dark,
The pit had been dug that bided its time.
In the pitch dark the feet felt for the ground
And pretended they found that pit nowhere.

Head bent, the mind thought 'twould
muzzle the heart
For certain 'twould fare better in the world
If it cancelled that rogue, wrote itself in,
To make certain love did submit nowhere.

The secret that was quite known yet unknown,
Acknowledged for gain, denied of its fear,
Could not die for they would not let it go,
Nor live for allowance was writ nowhere.

Fine green was the maze wherein it did live.
Greener its mind all the seasons it worked,
Gleaning and leaning on mem'ries beyond,
To escape, when was an exit nowhere.

Respite sought from on high achieved a hit,
And more whereof to partake then seemed meet.
Relief sought in acquiescence, and yet
They said, 'Seek it, you shall find it nowhere.'

ஃௐ

ഇ 83 ൙

New hope gave new life to each day and place
That beckoned the heart and yet there was seen
The face that killed heart and hope yesterday
That face in the day's market square was seen.

How did ten times, ten faces seem as one?
How was it done? The king and prince was he
Who lounged astreet with the same eyes of steel,
That signed trouble, whereof same stare was seen.

The chair needed fixing its wood was broke.
Woodworker away with his men in charge,
That mended the problem again all wrong,
In whose oft transgressions a snare was seen.

The heart was aging, where earlier its youth

Had fought its battles now lost and now
won.
Older eyes saw more to life than itself
And need for belief and for prayer was seen.

As the day turned in for the night instead
Of relief in its sleep restlessness knew:
The face of the child, the turn in its life,
Red ribbon long in blackened hair was seen.

Frail food to keep the old body alive,
Old heart with hands gnarled did cook for
the day,
Meagre meal, with mind in rheumy past if
Alive 'twould survive this howe'er was
seen.

Was the body aged so much as the mind,
Tired with reconciliation none
From fight that never seemed frail or e'en
weak,
And truce disbelieved for it ne'er was seen.

ৡଓ

ᤌ 84 ᤏ

Home beckoned when far off fires seemed
warm
Making the proud heart want to plan to
move,
When the mind's eye flashed pyres, the
heart thought
Staying here would be better than to move.

It sat in the market 'twixt the fat sacks
Coloured and grained, heart pale though
seen ignored,
Wherefrom amidst day's coloured survival
It first did safely search and scan to move.

Merchant quite busy, bound the sold
packets
Expertly with twine dangling from above,
Warily eying one crowding the crowds,
That surged 'twas then he asked the man to
move.

Feet in the dust, hand feeling few coins in
Yesterday's pocket, that would last a day,
No more, the next job, the next copper lot

The newly poor eyes had to pan to move.

If wanting meant getting, world would be mine,
All days captured, all of time would be fine,
But night passed fevered, and the day's dark dawn,
With God's mercy, slowly began to move.

A swing of the axe and the wood was cut.
In arc of the blade was new vision seen
Of the past that was called from future's past.
With drudge of the day came new ban to move.

The preferred were known that they played with love,
Won each time and hitting, apologised.
Most brilliant and able minds of their time.
God's love not left out in their plan to move.

ℰ 85 ℛ

The old man passed on and his death was mourned
When the new child asked what it meant to age,
In circle of things, life comes as it goes
And the world seems quite malcontent to age.

Garden by the stone font, the gardener grew,
Had flowers aplenty and regrets few,
When one arrived filled with hope and love new
The other had withered, relent to age.

Carvings of pages, their words stone engraved
Resisted weather as others did too
Made of earthly voicings, echoes, and prayers
Life ne'er allowed that document to age.

The time was the player and it played with hues
Red and blue, preaching one, eschewing

two.
Life the teacher, stopped play and stripped playthings
Of its student, who was then sent to age.

Though face had long lost the freshness of youth,
A weakness of spirit there found was none
When knee bent stood up to the step with strength,
Forgiveness of itself then leant to age.

What day of what past was left late who knew
Wither came memory and learning true.
What night must next dawn follow when rebirth
The final day did circumvent to age.

ಸ 86 ಇ

Encouragement died, support stepped aside,
'Twas time to stop work and fall ill again,
As heart had lain dying, when day forced work
That day was now dead. Time stood still again.

Would the page move on to pastures greener
And pick up each word anew from the start
Or search the last day's page already writ
And thence pick up the now dried quill again?

Tonight is the last. The voice had told it.
Lie down. Get ready to go with the night.
At some hour, rival was ta'en, and day dawned
Still live the hand reached for its pill again.

Why fool oneself with feelings of wisdom?
No one is all good, and not one all bad.
Just when next feeling gives into surprise

Wayward time turns to fit heart's bill again.

So where does life go, up to the heavens
On to the next shore, to earlier era,
Into folk lore, or back to new journey
To push on, constantly uphill again.

'Your death's delayed and 'twill be your turn soon,
Till then keep working the word on the loom,
Falling and praying, trying to stand up
Knowing naught's done against His will again.'

Hubris of the dead that stares from beyond:
Beyond the struggle, past the survival.
While days drag their feet through health and ill health,
Summer's heat turns shiver and chill again.

௣ 87 ௣

As long as in sleeping breast, breath did rise
Though life was spent, the heart did sough
onward.
The night skies rolled, the breeze blew, sun
brought life
That asked the heart near death to plough
onward.

Once there was plenty when plenty was
gi'en,
Hand freely received and handed it out,
For next while when dearth meant hoarding
expense,
'Twas felt 'caution's better from now
onward.'

One's creed was it, colour, or time and space
That put to world's edge its value and
worth?
Trust of the father made easier to bare
Whate'er end they did disendow onward.

If heart had no place, worth only given
To hands and to heights, then why did the

lord
Allow it to be born, why was it made
To struggle and live anyhow onward?

When the worst of life is given to ye
By one that creates, its reason belongs
To almighty's ken, accepted as such,
Used then that belief and know how onward.

In worst of lives, the sun did shine sometimes.
The flow'rs did bloom and heart turned with loving.
The head dear rheumed got replenished with strength,
Told faith, 'Step aside and allow onward.'

The mind said 'Choose poverty to get hit,
But stay within realms of the golden orb.'
The heart needed love of a free form world,
'It would be seen maybe, somehow, onward.'

ॐ

ॐ 88 ☙

Time stepped into dearth, into near death's phase
That syllable writ was the penult one.
End would come easy, maybe, but who knew?
Was this 'last but one' the difficult one?

Derided, by one dictated by Him
The head bent prayed for support against him
Who prayed near with equal ferve and faith,
To make known God though that did insult one.

Of the two, lord, who is it thou wilt chose?
Thou that knowest not wrath, but love 'tis known,
Though for safety the heart prays it knows ye
When thou exempts me, and does exult one.

Yet the foe that prayed for blessings transgressed,
Falsely repented, sought blessings anew.

Heart feared neighbour's new blessings would result
In the hit new that they did indult one.

When head is the heart, the poet sees that
It's bent its head to be hurt for it knows
To mistrust is the way of the child and
To trust despite raging the adult one.

Foe was helped, to lay on danger and hate
Making sure life was lead by taking care.
Foe was helped, but did the heart too not pray
And was saved for it turned to consult one?

Not easy to write, not easy to feel
The grace of the world in face of the foe.
Yet how large the mercy to love alike
Wherefrom it sufficed not to incult one.

ೞಚ

ॐ 89 ◌

From some miles away in the bazaar square
'Midst diff'rent faces that same face appeared.
Exotic wares manned from 'cross seas and lands
To barter, to keep up the chase appeared.

Gathered round tea stalls, heat warm in their palms,
Banal was discussed no less and no more.
Shadow moved 'cross wood quickly, sun crossed skies.
In their speech, in dealings no trace appeared.

Sun set to darkness so pitch as if burnt.
All seemed settled, asleep though nothing stirred.
Silence rent by string of barking then stopped.
Sinister stillness in its place appeared.

Next morn was still quiet for they all knew,
But knew not if to talk or keep it down.

By noon, the heat of the sun was clouded.
First traces of last night's disgrace appeared.

The stranger was gone yet stood in the crowd,
That people knew not whom they did deride.
Himself or his deeds to plead 'gainst his cause,
Dispel any doubt that in case appeared.

'Call me father, for in some years I'm dust.'
People warmed up to his friendly support.
Son's deeds discussed with their friend the father
While the other escaped, the ace appeared.

The crowd set aside one wrong in the throng,
Yet too young to partake in the Tsar's world.
The youth noted the stealth as they parted
That in the sworn friendships' embrace appeared.

₨₲

꧁ 90 ꧂

Love sowed seed elsewhere and lived of its
fruit
Ignorant, pretended in other life.
Aloof and detached when close to the
spawn.
Controlling from afar did father life.

Between wooden slats life crawled into
birth
Propped up by appendages of rough
growth
And feelers that sussed out each mood and
thought,
On that floor, the babe did know mother life.

The first cut, the first of its blood was shed
When the child pushed aground, and was
first bled,
To struggle, stand, first aching step
wherewith
'Twas conscripted till death for further life.

When through the fine mother the Lord did
love,

When each test was a lesson from above
When each bloody step did take to the hill,
To be born anew, but first murther life.

The written what seemed tragic, 'twas the truth
Not happy as other's, yet nothing new,
In black and white with no colours but brown
On paper, the poet did author life.

How did a poor life feel so full of love
And beauty of thankfulness of the blessed,
When two coins in its pocket bought dry bread
When finest of feasts did not bother life.

Yet for how long must one rough out the road
Watch from afar warmth of the kinfolk's sup
With father that left last one to the lord,
To choose want, know Him in another life.

ೱೲ

❧ 91 ☙

'Neath the high ceilings, lack of acceptance
With grace in that mansion pretension stayed
'Midst smooth floors, plush chairs and one ornate clock
For too long was quiet intention stayed.

A gash in the field exposed grey bare rocks
That yawned its darkness to counter the green
Persistant year long, as blot to the lush,
And danger therein that contention stayed.

White cottoned feelings felt and praised new silk,
That time forgot to engender some more,
Since it had not the lost shine of old gold
So then no more was reprehension stayed.

Sands on the plateau that had broken bits
Of shells, invites from seas somewhere afar.
Overun by familiar if strained ties,
Thus was movement with apprehension stayed.

It came overnight, the drop to near death,
The move down the mountain, through
twists and turns,
The scramble, return, new fall, all in hope
Of new place where new comprehension
stayed.

That one season when it rained and the leaf
Shook by the wind finally fell astream,
And was taken to sea, that day onward
From the tree forever its mention stayed.

Beyond the bazaar, wrong side of the road
Of no return, jostled by new feet far
From street of repute that still housed a self,
In new room, new wooden dimension
stayed.

Was it that diff'rent for fear was here too,
In each filthy nook stared each eye aflame.
There was fear wrapped in fine soft silk, and
here,
Open, uninhibited tension stayed.

❧❧

☧ 92 ☨

Dry bread, some cheese was the first street
meal brought,
And first new words learnt were 'Hands
hath no change.'
Sun set as always past the housing new,
And thus tired mind watched the shadow
change.

When bright coloured thread of life's work
was put
To the day's patch and its small needle's eye,
Wherewith many inexpert knots of toil
Were tried in fabric of fate to sew change.

Life learnt to recognise shadow that lurked
Watching it ever not letting it move.
Luck locked by the strong arm of law it
learnt
To remain the life that did not know change.

Which book said that long strides made up
the sum
And substance of life whereof wherewithal
Was enabled to begot through joys small,

That held life routine, but did elbow change.

'Thy pot's half full, but heart overfloweth.'
Voice from beyond said, 'Put paper to pen.'
Rhyme and refrain each light and dark with strength
Waxing and waning, would that rondeau change?

Strength without challenged dying strength within,
And fail it did, and reduced, but managed
To hang on when needed, learnt to let go
And thus enabled a sure, but slow change.

'Enough,' said fatigue, 'Put your pencil down.
How long can you write or interesting make
This life of dust made of toil not of gold
That stayed in one place and knew of no change.'

ॐ

ਞ 93 ಂ

Blame not the bazaar, folks, for it was made
For to trade, to upgrade, and to move on.
Discomfort of those that sat at the stalls
Did not last for they were manned to move
on.

Soft was the sunset, soothing in the breeze.
Length of the shadows said, 'Take it easy.'
Pitch of the dark said, 'The day was too frail.'
The foot did rest on the sands to move on.

Busy new mornings brought clatter of
meals,
Movement of people, the rush in the streets,
Meetings, guarantees, it watched for a while,
And then the heart felt too grand to move
on.

Friendships were made with those that
knew to whom
They were obligated, played to his tune:
'Twas the head that no longer supported
The heart that learnt beforehand to move on.
The bazaar did brawl, when each fist let fly,

When 'To punch, get punched' was accepted cry,
Step neatly aside when hit for the Heart
Nothing seemed too underhand to move on.

Cowardice to stay away or plain sense.
Pushed and insulted, the word was defence.
Coward they called that which picked up no fight
But then the pen stood its stand to move on.

The heart no fool knew of others through fight
That let the head rule, and took down the thought
Of itself beyond that marked for danger,
And the horizon it scanned to move on.

Like a star shot, past the dark native shore,
If heavenly quite brief in its note that
Just now appeared, and just now disappeared,
The call that came past the strand to move on.

℘ 94 ℘

Change failed to know its road with its end
marked,
Realised it better have travelled it.
If other's ways were well ruled, its own
spelt:
'Thou shalt not choose' thus had life titled
it.

To ensure that there was that brilliance none
Life's need repeated and thus death was
done.
The heart tripped happily down its own
path
Distress kept pace, made sure it rivalled it.

Was silence a scourge for it gave refuge
When to speak meant to endanger one's life
But then encouraged the heart spoke its
mind
Then wondered how well it had handled it.

When work was well trod then the luck did
strike
And path moved beneath the step that was

lit,
But before soon was life back to the ground,
When road reared saying, 'Thy fate hath bridled it.'

The hand that hit had not strength of the will
To tell them 'no', no matter what the cause
Under that drive was so much more achieved
With so much done few could have equalled it.

In destruction was creation achieved
For heights of worth not made from sound of base,
Yet with new birth unseen, first strike was felt
New knowledge born hadn't unsettled it.

What lay ahead the road of twists and turn,
When all one wanted was a day of peace,
Instead given moment's exaltation,
Which next turn its fate then hath humbled it.

❦❧

ॐ 95 ॐ

The fevered year lay down when time was done,
And death crossed its face, the next day arose.
Although the night was cold and still in bed
The sun that lit the onward way arose.

If the next day stayed back it knew it would
No longer have heart to participate.
Gaze dark and mind busy with storms beyond,
Restlessness with no cause to stay arose.

'Arise,' the voice said, 'Let time be not done.'
This world doth need thee not no more, but move,
For in the next awaits the rising sun.'
Though the Heart still unsure, did sway, arose.

'What was achieved other than facing strife
Wherewith how hath the world been better left
For it having lived at all, learnt and died.'

Such questions that did a ton weigh arose.

And yet, what pride to say that this was all.
To limp out the seemingly lasting fall
To pick up briefly delayed prospect gay
Moment that would not stay at nay arose.

Like that earlier time when death had risen
To a life new, when the riens of the ride
Were ta'en again to meet the past foe that
Newly made next slight to repay arose.

But for this moment was life dead and cold,
With movement none, but in the feet of
folks,
Strangers that sat till time it was to take
It to its resting place when they arose.

₨ 96 ⅚

By the barrels, that the fruiterer sold
For a coin a piece were the melons kept,
Near by, seeming free, for no cost at all
Was the enslaved by the castellan kept.

The heart had its currency which could be
Counted not to castle climb or barter,
But used to make self strong, last out each storm
'Twas deep within in form of billon kept.

'Art thou free, thinks thyself not supported,
But, in truth, thy mere pittance doth enslave.'
The heart after some lifetime of wand'ring,
Settled down like 'twas of the pollen kept.

The road was companion and still went on
Bereft of beating, bereaved of its soul,
It thought, but turned not to town to see if
Its friend was dead or like a felon kept.

Heart was fevered, but cool winds of the road

Would cure it till its path drove it back home
To fall ill again, look out past the seas,
To yearn to be more than a villien kept.

'This is where thou wilst remain till thy death,
Search not for new vistas where there be none.'
Even so 'twould get on a ship and leave
Were not the west wind by the villain kept.

And so sat silent heart in the village square
Watching the longing, never belonging,
Hanging on to its nerve somewhere somewhen
Was the last dreg of strength like stolen kept.

In worldly prison bars one did not see
Held there entirely free by lack of love
Like the tyrant's rule, was the fool, the heart
Forever schooled like homeless Arian kept.

ॐ

ೞ 97 ೪

The south winds blew the trees, firmament swayed,
Heavens fell to disorient the skies.
Quick light of beyond then bathed the world
As vehement battery rent the skies.

The light and silence, the darkness and sounds:
Raining of heavenly wrath spent the earth
That waited tension of next heaven torn,
When dread of rupture did torment the skies.

Night was as dark and as near to the nether
And the next moment was night as the day,
But brilliant more and nearer to the north:
What transformation underwent the skies.

For three whole days the rains would not relent,
Folks stayed within as nature played without.
Someone being punished somewhere for

their deeds,
Being hit and forced to repetend the skies.

Until the master did the sinner school,
World of water stayed past a water's screen,
That subsided, then increased, but indoors,
To some subdued work, the hours lent the
skies.

The storm should end, it would, finally did.
The folks came out chastened to do their
work,
In the world washed out, yet blue, and quiet,
Grateful for what now did absent the skies.

So, that day the season changed from the
one
That had grown too harsh to handle for all.
That day then stepped back, was made to let
go
As for this day the last forewent the skies.

༄༈

ೞ 98 ೞ

Never stay, but away to lands afar
To move, to travel, to pursue the verb,
But when the heart at its purpose stood
stuck
At phrase's end, it sat down to the verb.

Not of skin, but of soul its meaning made
With shades aplenty as many as minds.
Some so far off from the point when 'twas
read
That it made one wonder who knew the
verb.

Drab heart's need the world politely
declined
When to smart mind they made their needy
plea.
Same spell caught next day that agreed to
'Life',
But in new light, heart did review the verb.

Stop not the heart for the lord at its birth
Did nominate the next when with it came
Its duty to take it one at a time

And then create in that ague the verb.

They said that verse is quarrel with the self
And use not quality of rhyme to rage.
The pen set words to blame, and if it could,
Caught its mistake and then withdrew the
verb.

Words hath no strength, and when nerves
became not
New verses, when cut short, and maimed
by life
That ached, abused the pen to write their
woes,
Then, how often did anger cue the verb?

Amongst numbers count thyself that have
not
Case of birth, and so with commas count
days,
With periods of rest apace to recoup
When lack will let thee then onto the verb.

ಌ 99 ಞ

Days by its seconds marked when sun arose
It was the day of the market by then.
The fine folks from high were being
welcomed watched
By bunting that cared not to quit by then.

Face aface self pretended not to know,
Said, 'It's you, is it?' graciously and then
Moved on for it knew that with this meeting
Ragged strength, pretence had been hit by
then.

Onslaught of nerves bought cubeb and
ptisan
And the day moved away back dark
indoors
Where work waited knowledge that it could
not
Move back up it had to admit by then.

That was then, this is now, then you were
there,
Now they're there not near the meagre
that's yours.

Lord's plan that had seemed too harsh and too cruel
Through struggling acceptance was lit by then.

'If thou wert all good and they wert all free,
How easy would life's and Lord's judgement be,
If like you, he hated them, but loved thee.'
Each thought arrived lacking in wit by then.

By evening were all deals done, and wares sold.
When the heart came out to the empty mart
And looked up at the painted sun whereon
Had nature's love used its palette by then.

The next day would dawn and next attempt made
To work the till held by the hand from far.
Meal earned, heart exhausted looked to some rest,
But ensured day's word would be writ by then.

ℬℭ

ಸ 100 ಣ

Though in final hour, the heart was still
young
Looked above with no knowledge of the
soul.
It felt in laboured day heavy its dream,
But knew therein life and thereof the soul.

With shade aplenty, shelter to the world
When the tree was physic to weakened leaf
Dropped for reasons beyond unknown,
'twas told
And thence unknown the sense hereof, the
soul.

Not of the father, neither to the son,
Yet through the gift of praise its race was
run,
And glimpse of earlier life quite useless
seen,
But then was seen in place whereof the soul.

And that was when the song ran out of
rhyme.
End not reached, it needed to end its time,

Words strung quite senselessly sung quite
off tune
Changed in between yet onward strove the
soul.

Under the tree the more the Sacristan
Denied the hungry mouth the crust the
more
To plan divine cleaved the heart and its life
To the heavens that further drove the soul.

'Pray to the mountains,' for score years it
did,
Till pain of the climb turned call of the page,
That offered itself no strictures of birth
That let heart to find in its trove, the soul.

Nothing writ these pages can be termed
good,
And bad can never be that which it deemed.
The phrases did end the journey did not,
Lived on in way that did behove the soul

ೲ

ఙ 101 ఞ

In streets, on scraps, burnt out words of the
sun
With the day 'twas thought that the tale
would end.
Soon the story made of wood, lost and
found
And small in stomach of the whale would
end.

The bazaar began and people appeared
Hearty and hale as each business bargained,
And made sure that nothing got in its way
And that day with more bread and ale
would end.

Thus the bazaar sustained each day and
next,
Like the shadows past twilight's veil did
move.
The bird as it hopped the grain on the
ground,
Knew that its life beyond its pale would end.

Cobbled street lined with the abandoned

shops
On each side once manned by voices that
said,
'Walk, if you will, saying 'you don't belong',
By waters it could be your trail would end.'

Steps to the river submerged in each wave
Would be lost to eyes soon as night was
nigh,
But shout from somewhere and the barge
was seen,
Or else how could it be this gaol would end.

By sounds of the temple, its bells and chants
Heart arose, unsteady, feeling the sway.
If it lasted this out it thought maybe
Painful stain of the ancient nail would end.

Ha, with what dost thou ail, how art thou
frail?
Nature hath not time for any of this.
It moveth suns and moons, and knows from
past,
In time, the worst infant's worst wail would
end.